EATING

&

PRAYING

EATING

&

PRAYING

DAVIS SUMMERS

atmosphere press

"Nothing's lost forever. In this world, there's a kind of painful progress. Longing for what we've left behind, and dreaming ahead. At least I think that's so."

Tony Kushner, *Angels in America*

Chapter One

Tyler Morgan had never expected to have his heart broken on a Tuesday. Tuesdays were all about business, cold and structured. Heartbreaks were messy, a roiling pot of emotions—something to endure on a weekend. Especially if one had to confront the blinding hangover that had now overtaken Tyler. There was no doubting it: Leo had left him. But couldn't he at least have given Tyler's assistant a heads-up? Amber could have scheduled the heartache and saved Tyler all this mid-week misery. Instead, he sat alone in his apartment—the apartment he had shared with Leo!—and shook from a rush of adrenaline. The breakup had happened so suddenly. It was as if his mind had just begun to process the shock his body was already experiencing. The soft hairs in his inner ear had absorbed the overflow of alcohol, amplifying his tinnitus to a piercing pitch. Tornado sirens, he thought—his head blared at the same frequency as those sirens from his youth. Where had everything gone wrong?

Through the fog, Tyler could see how all the signs of a foreboding breakup were there.

Leo had been sorting through his belongings for weeks—maybe months—and Tyler hadn't even thought to notice. Leo had removed the downtown artist's portrait of Demi Lovato, a painting inspired by an unflattering paparazzo shot. The bookshelf was cleared of Leo's favorite titles, including the first edition copy of *Pretty Little Liars*, a quasi-ironic gift to commemorate a television series they quasi-ironically binged. Even the unwashed extra set of Boll & Branch sheets that had sat in the corner of the foyer for months was removed—Tyler hadn't been home enough to pick up on it. Two stuffed duffle bags were the last of Leo's possessions, and they, too, went out the door with him.

"Tyler, I'm leaving you."

Those were Leo's words. So definite. So absolute. Tyler didn't even know what to think—at first. His mouth opened and he wore an incredulous half-grin. "What?"

"I'm leaving, Tyler."

"But—but *why!*" he cried, reality setting in. "I don't understand."

He did his best not to slur his words. His nightly after-work outing had devolved into several rounds of gin and tonics with friends. The acid in his stomach churned the cocktails, prompting spasms deep inside him. He collapsed to the floor and found himself crawling on his hands and knees toward Leo, begging him not to go. Tyler suddenly thought of the scene in *Sunset Boulevard* in which Norma Desmond begs her younger lover not to leave her palatial lair. Tyler had loved her extravagance, the camp of Gloria Swanson's performance, but here he was now, beseeching his lover, on his knees, and this shit was in no way amusing.

"Look at you, Tyler. I don't even know the last time I saw you laugh! Or kiss me! Or tell me you love me!"

"I *love* you," Tyler pleaded. He reached out to Leo. "I love you!"

Leo wasn't having it. "We have no relationship," he said, exasperated. "And we haven't for a long time. And what about the future? I've known you for four years, and it's clear you don't care about me. You come home wasted every night. I mean, falling-down, get-some-fucking-help, full-blown-drunk. *Every night!* And when you're not drunk, you're working. Or you're drunk *and* working. And all for what? To produce some little movies that a bunch of Letterboxd-obsessed teens watch? You're a *shell* of the man you used to be."

That word hit especially hard. *Shell.* It made Tyler sound

like a dried-out carcass. *Whoa!* Sure, he was getting older, and on some days he desperately needed moisturizer, but now he couldn't get the image of a wrinkled Mother Teresa out of his head. He looked up into Leo's emotionless eyes.

"I—I don't know what to do... Leo! You can't do this!"

"I loved you, Tyler. I loved you so much. But I don't anymore. And you don't love me either. You'll see. You just need some distance."

Leo turned the doorknob and pulled the door open. The hallway's ghastly fluorescent lighting burned into the dark apartment.

"I will do *anything*. Leo! Please. Please just give me a chance! You can't end it like this!"

"You made this decision for us long ago. I'm just the one who's going to see it through. I hope you get what you need."

And with that, he closed the door.

• • •

The next hours seemed impossibly long, measured only by P!nk's *"Just Like a Pill,"* which Tyler kept replaying on his stereo as he lay on the floor in the foyer. On the nose, yes, but the song conveyed everything Tyler was wrestling with that night. It wasn't supposed to hurt like this. He was proud, almost indignant, about how little he needed from Leo, emotionally. That was part of the draw. His career was in chaos, but he was able to come home every night to the one thing in his life that was stable: that six-foot swimmer he fell in love with all those seasons ago.

Now, the breakup spelled an uncertain future. All those dreams he and Leo had ceased to exist. The summer house in Woodstock they talked about buying. The vacations to Bora Bora.

Having children—they even went over names that they liked. All gone. This gutting of possibility was what ripped through Tyler's body, leaving him unable to move.

When Tyler's phone died, drained by P!nk's incessant heartbreak, he didn't dare plug it in. He was afraid to see that the world had carried on without him while he was immobilized on the floor. The days passed, and Tyler drew the curtains throughout the apartment, sealing himself in his misery. He got by on microwaved popcorn and frozen pierogies, letting them barely thaw in the oven before pulling them out with his bare hands. Bathing was the first daily routine to fall by the wayside. Tyler also found himself no longer speaking. He didn't utter a word after Leo shut the front door. He wondered what it'd be like never to speak again. How loud his life had become over the past several years. How loud he had become. Maybe there was something to it, the quiet. As quickly as the thought entered his mind, it left. *Ding!* His tinny door bell made him jump. *Ding!*

He stood frozen in the living room, scared of who could be on the other side of the door. The bell rang a third time, followed by a fist rapping on the solid wood of the door. *Oh my God*, he thought. *It must be Leo*! But wouldn't Leo have his key? Maybe he left it behind, too proud to take it with him. A key found its way into the lock and turned. *I really need to find a therapist and get this drinking under control*, he thought, his hopes rising. He would finally figure out a work-life balance. He would make it work with Leo. He was ready!

But it wasn't Leo who stood in the doorway. It was Alexa. He was ashamed. His physical appearance had deteriorated during the past few days, but he had also fooled himself into believing that Leo might actually come back to him. It had felt like just a few weeks ago when Alexa stood in that very spot, helping Leo and him move into the apartment almost three years earlier. Tyler stubbornly refused to hire professional movers, insisting that he possessed the physical strength and the friendships required to move unassisted in New York City. Alexa was assigned the thankless task of lifting the boxes out of the U-Haul, then carrying them up the four flights of stairs to the apartment door where Tyler, lofty as ever, had ordained himself with the mighty task of opening boxes and occasionally unpacking them. The three christened the apartment that day, passing around some indica that Tyler had brought back the previous week from work in Los Angeles, where he had begged (and failed) to acquire Lea Michele's life rights for a biopic. Settled down by the marijuana, they rested their exhausted bodies on the hardwood floor, reveling in the cool of the overworked window unit. Dehydrated and soaked in sweat—it was Tyler's brilliant idea to move in Manhattan in godawful August, when everyone they knew had the sense to be on Fire Island—they wolfed down some delivered pad Thai, accompanied by a middling bottle of rosé. Tyler thought the free meal was sufficient compensation for an entire day's work. Alexa didn't complain, knowing that Tyler would probably return the favor—if she asked when he was in the right mood. Three years later, Alexa stood at that same doorway, letting herself in to help her helpless friend yet again.

"Are you okay? Why haven't you called!" Alexa rushed into the living room with the urgency of a best friend. She extended her arms around his shoulders, hugging him for what felt like minutes. Tyler had forgotten how good it could feel to be embraced.

"Talking about this would have made it real," he said. "And I really don't want it to be real." He tucked his head under her arm.

"Honey, I know you live your life all *out of sight, out of mind,* but that just might not be the best way of handling a major crisis." She was right, Tyler knew. He had gotten pretty far while keeping his skeletons buried in a closet—that one in the corner would serve as an apt metaphor, its mess of linens forever pressing up against the door. There was a certain shame in secrecy, but there was an even greater shame in denial.

"How did you know?"

"Your phone kept going straight to voicemail. So I called Leo. And he told me." Tyler kept his head snuggled under her arm.

"How did he sound?"

"He sounded heartbroken, Tyler." This soothed him. He

had imagined Leo happily gallivanting about town, a man once again on the make, freed from his tormentor.

"What do you need?" Alexa asked.

"I say this with my entire being: I don't know."

"That's perfectly understandable," she said. "But what are you going to do?" He looked at her.

"I have no idea. It's too much *him*, even with all his shit gone. I can see him everywhere, and I can't take it."

There was something else, something he was too embarrassed to admit: losing the apartment would mean losing the lifestyle he had grown accustomed to. Sure, Tyler made pretty good money, especially compared to the paltry sums that so many of his contemporary millennials loved to complain about online. But he had grown to rely on Leo's financial stability. The apartment would be ludicrous to pay for on just his salary alone—it was already over-budget for Leo and him as a couple.

"Please," said Alexa. "No more hiding. If you need something, just ask. Okay? And no more hiding. I found out: you're single. No shame." She collected her purse from the coffee table, where she had tossed it.

"Off so soon?" Tyler asked.

"Well, now that I know you aren't dead, I'm going to get home to my own life. Call me."

"Okay, love you."

"I love *you*," said Alexa, closing the door behind her.

Tyler felt lucky to have Alexa in his corner, no matter the circumstances. He saw so many people around him who were truly alone—no friend, no lover, no child, no family. So many other friends had come and gone: there was Blair, his freshman roommate at NYU. The two had been fast friends, terrorizing the city together, never saying no to an open bar or an open bottle of poppers. They would harmonize lesser-known Reba McEntire songs and watched *The Real Housewives of New York City* every week with the fervor of devoted congregants.

And then they slowly drifted apart. Blair had always been a bit unstable. He'd have one drink too many and pick a fight with random strangers. And so Tyler kept his distance, and soon they stopped speaking altogether. There were so many other friends with promising beginnings and fizzled out endings that Tyler couldn't possibly remember them all.

With Alexa gone, the silence was far from comforting; it felt suffocating. He had no immunity against the quiet. He felt drained and was pale and beaded with sweat. He grabbed his Tumi purse from the ottoman and scavenged through it for the Xanax bottle.

Shit! He forgot to call his doctor's office for a refill. The room began to contort and lengthen while his chest grew heavier. The dreaded, familiar yellow spots began to cloud his vision, and his knees buckled. He pressed his forehead into the floor in something like a child pose, arms stretched out in front of his body. He shuddered as he gasped for air, eyes closed. He was desperate to find some semblance of breath. Missouri tornado sirens blared in his ears. The ringing continued to build as his anxiety swelled. Until ... silence.

• • •

Speak.

He heard it so clearly.

Speak.

The voice was familiar. Tiny, yet still familiar. Was it his own?

Speak.

Uh, God? Hello? It's been a long time. And I'm sorry about that. But I could use your help. Actually, I desperately need your help. Please. I've never felt so lost in my life. Nothing is right. I can't keep going on like this. You probably know that already. I need Leo. I need him more than anything else, God. He's my everything, and now he's gone. And now I feel completely lost. So please, God, I'm asking for some guidance. Because, uh, because, I just really need a sign, please. I know, I know, you haven't heard from me in a while, and this is such a needy request. So, thank you? Uh, goodbye for now. Oh, right. I should say "amen," right? So... Amen.

Where the fuck did that come from? He hadn't ended up in a prayer-like pose on purpose—it was his anxiety's doing. But before he knew it, the words were coming forth, not even concealed within the privacy of his own thoughts. They were spoken aloud: a definite call upon the Energies of the Universe for some divine intervention. What did he even know about prayer? He was raised Southern Baptist, but it was more of a community gathering spot for other families in his hometown of Dexter, Missouri. Nothing more than some free babysitting on Sunday mornings and Wednesday nights. He grew up reciting the Lord's Prayer and other archaic, hollow ramblings, of course, but Tyler had never spoken *directly* to God. At least not that he knew of.

Waiting for something, anything, Tyler opened his eyes and pulled himself up to his knees. The anxiety had released its choking grip from around his throat. Dust and crumbs from the unswept floor were pressed into his cheeks. He wiped the residue away and placed his hands on his hips, finally able to take in deep breaths.

Finding the strength to stand up, Tyler walked over to the couch and slid into its comforting cushions. Finally, some relief. He picked up his lifeless phone, resuscitating it by plugging it into the nearest socket. He was desperate to play some Doodle Jump—the best way to recover after one of his attacks. In the process, he saw a notification on the Facebook app. How gauche! Why did he even still have Facebook? It's not like he was just dying to know his aunt Tina was promoting alt-right conspiracies that Alexandria Ocasio-Cortez was trafficking children on behalf of the Bidens and Obamas. Nevertheless intrigued—*ironically!*, he insisted to himself—he clicked on the app and saw the notification was a memory from ten years ago. He tapped on the notification. It was a photograph. There he stood, ten years ago, in all his nineteen-year-old, one-hundred-and-twenty-five-pound glory—with his mom. Oh, Mom, he thought, she was so beautiful. They stood under a marquee whose bright, red letters read *EAT PRAY LOVE – PREMIERE – 8 PM*, both pointing up with cheesy smiles reaching across their faces. The photo was from the 2010 Traverse City Film Festival, which his family attended every summer during their three-week stays at his grandmother's lakeside cabin in Leland, Michigan. The place allowed the family to have a free little vacation between the farming season (which kept his father away most of the year, thankfully) and the upcoming school year. Two thousand and ten was his last year to join his parents in Michigan as he was leaving for NYU the following week. He and his mother were so thrilled by the idea of maybe meeting Julia Roberts that they stood in a standby line for six hours, begging passers-by for tickets.

Tyler felt a pang in his chest and clicked out of the app, afraid of what might come.

The movie had sparked a watershed moment in American culture. He remembered it so clearly. Women left their families, their careers, and their homes, all in the name of transformation—desperate for a taste of what Julia Roberts experienced in bringing Elizabeth Gilbert's memoir to the big screen. It had enraptured him as a teenager, the Oprah-ness of it all. He saw himself so clearly in that story, even if he was an unmarried, underweight twink reared in America's heartland. It was a time of unmatched change, unmatched possibility. There was a tangible hope that spread throughout the land. Years later, when Tyler would dabble in ancient Jewish mysticism at the Kabbalah Centre (thanks to Madonna's *Ray of Light*), he couldn't help but feel connected to that moment in which so many women had started over. There was something so resonant about Elizabeth Gilbert's story. His heart skipped a beat and he gasped—the signature gay gasp! *Wait a minute.* This was it. *Oh my God—God!* This was the sign he prayed for!

Chapter Two

"What? You're re-creating *Eat Pray Love*?"

Yes, he was re-creating *Eat Pray Love*. Well, perhaps "re-create" was the wrong word for his planned expedition. Tyler was going to take an extended trip in the name of finding himself *inspired* by *Eat Pray Love*. That's the word he was searching for: *inspired*. Having worked in the minefields of film known as adaptations, Tyler was quite familiar with what jargon could be used to justify "inspired" pieces of art without having to legally clear anything. So there he was, about to embark on a global trip inspired by *Eat Pray Love*. Yes, he knew it sounded absolutely ridiculous. Yes, he knew it sounded unbearably banal. But he also knew that this was what he was being led to do. It appeared as if the *pray* portion was already working wonders for him.

Having been exalted on all fours only twelve hours earlier, the world seemed to open up to him as if for the first time. Never before had he felt such limitless potential in his future. Drowning in the routine of his life, he had been too afraid, or complacent, to ask for help. And so he reached out to Alexa. After all, she had just told him to call if he needed her—although she probably didn't imagine he'd be waking her up early the next morning. Now here she was, sitting across from him at a cafe, sleepy-eyed, for sure, but mouth agape in shock, incredulous that her friend suddenly wanted to leave town because of a 2010 romantic drama.

The night before was a blur of excitement and divine

adrenaline. Thankfully, Tyler wasn't the first brokenhearted soul to turn to Elizabeth Gilbert for guidance. A quick Google search turned up a seemingly endless stream of blogs, listicles, and Jezebel articles devoted to women who had followed in Gilbert's footsteps to heal their own wounds. One piece in particular caught his eye: *Eating and Praying and Loving on My Own Terms*. It was written by a bright-eyed and freshly highlighted Ashleigh Windham. The name sounded familiar—or was it Ashley he knew?

Or Kelly? He had a hard time distinguishing between all those publicists. He clicked on the article.

Namaste, my lovelies. I am truly blessed to have such an open-hearted following of #SpiritualWarriors. So, I would like to start this piece in a state of gratitude. I am grateful to you, yes YOU, for reading this. I'm grateful for G-d, and all that She has opened my eyes to. And most of all, I'm grateful to myself: for allowing myself to go through the open-soul surgery that was my voyage around the world. Now, I know what you must be thinking: quitting your job to travel the world to find yourself is the definition of privilege. And you're correct. I acknowledge that. But I also acknowledge that you can begin your own journey of transformation ANYWHERE: at your home, at your family's home, or at your family's summer home. I would also like to acknowledge the only thing preventing you from your own spiritual growth is YOU. This was the realization I came to six months ago when I logged on to Twitter one day to find out I had been wrongfully canceled (and I will NOT be addressing that Halloween costume ever again!). Never before had I been confronted with such hateful trolling. But it is my job, nay, my duty, as someone on a quest of spiritual enlightenment to rise above this hatred and vitriol. And so I, like the Great Taylor Swift, removed myself from the narrative. I did what I thought was the impossible and deactivated all my socials. I knew that the only way I would ever find that badass woman warrior inside of me was to completely disappear into myself. Knowing that I needed some time alone, I rented a bungalow at the Chateau Marmont, knowing my privacy would be respected there. Looking through the bookshelf in my bungalow, I stumbled on Eat Pray Love. Little did I know that this book would soon become my sacred text. I devoured it. That night, I checked out of my bungalow, called an Uber, and found myself standing at the international kiosk at LAX, purchasing a one-way ticket to Rome. This impulsiveness was an entirely new sensation. My entire life had been so organized: Mondays I shot content for my 1.25 million YouTube subscribers, Tuesdays I shot pics for my 3.5 million Instagram followers, Wednesdays were the days I spent with my dogs, Thursdays were TikTok development days where I storyboarded new ideas with my creative assistants, and Fridays were my shoot days for TikTok. My life was scheduled down to the minute, and yet, I HAD to leave it all behind. My time in Italy was when I learned to let go of my need to control. I let go of my diet. I let go of my need to be known. I let go of shaving my legs— HOLLA at my fellow European beauties! And when I let go, I let in God, in all Her glory. And She brought me the most incredible Italian men who taught me what it meant to love my body, and have my body be LOVED. And then I went to India with a new knowledge: I CAN take up space as a woman. Not only can I do it—I DESERVE to take up space. And in Bali—oh, Bali—I found true love for the first time. Yes, I fell in love. I was as shocked as you are. But this time it's for real. I never knew what it meant to be loved, to be SEEN by someone so intimately, so honestly. And so here I am: truly whole again. What I learned in Bali is that I needed only MYSELF to complete me. And Patrick M. (I can't reveal his full identity, of course) was just the man to teach me that. I met him on the beach one day, unable to take my eyes off him. What was intended to be a one-night stand (OMG, sorry Mom!!!) blossomed into a fully realized expression of love. And what are the chances that he works in finance in Los Angeles! Now that I'm back, we are seeing each other almost daily, unable to shake the newfound lease on life we discovered thousands of *miles away on that Indonesian island of perfection. I encourage each and every one of you to give yourselves the permission to live life! The permission to let God work Her magic and bless you with the fruits of your desires! I would not be the woman I am today had I not stumbled upon that life-changing book all those months ago at the Chateau Marmont, forever to be remembered as the birthplace of my own life-changing journey. Allow God to do some work in your lives, ladies. She knows EXACTLY what you need.*

Bless you. XX A.W.

P.S. Don't forget to check my "Shopping" link, which has great deals on assorted merch.

Tyler closed out of the piece. He was moved. Sure, it was trite and masturbatory, but it also spoke to something he wanted to hear: the possibility of change. He took comfort in knowing how familiar his experience was to so many others his age. He felt that there could be an answer to his suffering. It was possible to be happy!

He called Amber, clueless as to how inappropriate it was to call an assistant after midnight for a personal request. He unloaded all his baggage on her, and she listened patiently. To herself, she thought, *Thank you, God, this is just the vacation I need from Tyler.* After the call, she booked his journey in a matter of minutes.

"You're the best assistant I've ever had," he told her afterward, repeating the line he had used on his seven previous assistants, all of whom had quit on him. Tyler didn't mind seeing his assistants come and go. What mattered was that he kept making movies.

He smiled as his inbox lit up with Amber's forwarded emails of plane reservations and hotel accommodations. He would make some calls and escalate her quickly—his farewell gesture to the industry. She would inevitably go on to win some major award and cite that moment in her career as her "breakthrough," owing everything to Tyler and XYZ Productions. He would write a brief, heartfelt email saying he always knew she had what it took to get to the top.

Alexa was still coming to terms with her friend's overnight epiphany. "So, what are you going to do about your job?" she asked, her mouth still open in disbelief.

"I quit," Tyler said, casually sipping his iced tea.

"Tyler, you have to be joking."

"I'm as serious as a heart attack."

"But... But—*why*?" She flung up her hands and nearly knocked his tea off the table.

"*Because*... I'm just about where Elizabeth Gilbert was! She was near thirty, with the perfect job and perfect relationship—"

"Leo left you. What's perfect about that?"

"I said 'seemingly'!"

"No, actually you didn't!"

"*Anyway!* I'm where she was, and she had the foresight to get away from her life, to have a clear vision of the life she *wanted*. And that's what I need more than anything. I don't want this job. I don't want this town. I don't want this life! At least not for now. So, I'm going to re-create *Eat Pray Love*."

"What the hell do you even mean by *re-create*?"

"Well, it's not a shot-for-shot re-creation—more like a spiritual one. I'm going to spend one month in Italy, one in India, and then a final one in Bali. And it is going to be *so* healing." The waiter arrived to deliver their lunch salads, breaking the intensity of their eye contact. They shuffled their utensils as the waiter laid their orders before them.

"Baby, the entire point Elizabeth Gilbert was trying to make is that you can do what she did *anywhere*. You don't have to *literally* go to the same places she went to, all the while expecting to learn some miraculous wisdom!"

"Why not? Seriously, Alexa. Why the fuck not? It clearly worked for her! And then she got a bestselling book deal out of it *and* a box office smash! I would kill for those kinds of returns!" He poked at the salmon plated in front of him. Alexa yielded ever so briefly, absentmindedly smoothing the creases in the linen napkin folded on her lap.

"It just feels like you're so … *definite* about the whole thing."

"Exactly, Alexa! *Exactly.* I feel like this is the first time I've decided something for my life. I've been so passive."

It was true. Passivity was nothing new to Tyler Morgan. Hadn't his entire career more or less just happened to him? After graduating from NYU with a meaningless degree in communications (he got a full ride, thanks to his rural roots), Tyler was put up by Trent, a terribly tall and bland figure destined to be one of the ghosts of boyfriends past. Trent even landed Tyler his gig of covering a junior manager's desk at XYZ when it was a startup production company. Tyler had never expressed any interest in pursuing film and television production, but, hey, it was something to do! How was Tyler to know that this startup would become such a success in the independent film industry? Or that his then-boss Jason would rise to become the CEO, bringing Tyler along for the ride as an executive? Or that his own elevation in the company would drive off Trent in a fit of jealousy, his boyfriend a lowly writer's assistant on a soon-to-be-canceled streamer series? But once he was settled in at XYZ, Tyler discovered how ambitious he could be. Within little time, he was credited with sourcing six of the company's most successful films. He was making a name for himself, landing on thirty-under-thirty lists by age twenty-five. And yet Tyler still had a hard time acknowledging his success. At awards shows and parties and mixers, nothing made him more uncomfortable than hearing a stranger list his accomplishments—the accolades always sounded foreign, as if they were meant for another person. Invariably, he'd chuckle and shy away, heading to the bar for another gin and tonic.

"So," Alexa said, "what are you going to do for work when you get back?"

"What other twenty-nine-year-old has *six* features and a miniseries under his belt? *Someone* will want to hire me!"

"Sounds like you've got it all figured out, Tyler. I suppose all I can say is *buona fortuna!*"

. . .

Tyler stood in his emptied apartment, a relationship's worth of memories packed and taped shut in cardboard boxes sent to storage. He would travel light, taking with him only one checked suitcase, a carry-on, and his Birkin—a gift from a beloved agent who owed him one. The rest had been sorted, marked, labeled, and packed for him to sort through in three months, when he returned to America. It'd be much easier to deal with all the physical shit post-transformation, he thought. Fully prepared for his quest, there was only one thing left he needed to do. He went out into the unnaturally temperate May night and walked north up Clinton, crossing Houston, and continued up Avenue B. Arriving at Seventh Street, he made a left and headed west until arriving at the intersection of Seventh and Avenue A. He put in his AirPods, scrolled through his music library, and played Neil Young's "Harvest Moon."

Tyler and Leo had been dating for a month. Leo finally invited him over to meet Mary and Brian, his two closest friends. They were painfully boring, and the only thing they seemed to have in common was a shared enthusiasm for Shania Twain. They decided to go dancing at Niagara Bar, a stale, sweaty pit of twenty-somethings thrashing their limbs about. But the place did have an excellent DJ. Once inside, they made their way to the dance floor at the back of the bar, past the photo booths and the FiDi bros in Vineyard Vines screaming at the bartenders for Vodka Redbulls. Tyler laughed as Leo did his best to keep up with the music—he wasn't the most coordinated boyfriend he'd ever had. Leo's dance would start in his too-long swimmer arms, then slowly make its way up his spine until it was reduced to a simple side-to-side head bop. The bops weren't exactly on the beat, but rather *near* the beat. His awkwardness made Tyler's chest swell all the more, unable to keep his hands off of Leo. Tyler grabbed him and pulled him off the dance floor and into a photo booth. It was a secret dream of his to have a strip of pictures showing him and a boyfriend in one of the booths, mugging for the camera and kissing. It was that hetero, rom-com image of love so deeply ingrained. Smiling at their printed photo strip, Leo put his arm around Tyler, and the two made their way to the street to catch their breath.

Leaning into one another, they looked up. Playing from a nearby open-air restaurant was *Harvest Moon*. Leo extended his hand, and Tyler didn't miss a beat. There, at the corner of Seventh and Avenue A, with leafy Tompkins Square Park as a backdrop, they swayed under a glowing streetlight. Tyler looked up at Leo. Tears were forming in his eyes.

Come a little bit closer
Hear what I have to say
Just like children sleepin'
We could dream this night away

"Hey," said Tyler.

"Hey," said Leo. Tyler's mouth widened into a smile. Leo's expression softened. They held their gazes, holding each other tight.

"I love you," said Tyler for the first time.

Leo gave in, his tears flowing.

"I love you, too," he said, finally. "I love you, Tyler. I love you." And they kept dancing.

• • •

Tyler stood before his bags, having returned from his nostalgic outing. His Uber was arriving in two minutes. This plan that had felt so far away, so improbable, was now unfolding. He took one last look at what was soon to be his former home. He breathed deeply, determined to hold on to memories of the place. The love, the laughter, the fights, the tears—and the dust, the roaches, and the mice. All of it. It had all happened so quickly. How had four years slipped by? The days, the weeks, the years, all arriving at this very moment. Just days earlier, his heart had been broken in the spot where he now stood. And yet that felt like a distant time, too.

"Okay," he whispered. "I'm ready."

Chapter Three

The Italian air was intoxicating. Inhaling deeply, Tyler thanked the stewardesses and captains as he descended the stairs onto the tarmac. He felt as giddy as Audrey Hepburn, basking in the midday sun, ivory Globe-Trotter carry-ons in each hand. He had arrived!

The flight had gone by without a hitch. Accustomed to international travel after his years in the film industry, Tyler breezed through the TSA pre-check as if he were entering Bloomingdale's. Applying and obtaining Global Entry was his most-prized investment—next to the rose quartz energy-balancing water bottle recommended by GOOP, Gwyneth having cited its healing properties in helping her through a *terribly* public divorce. But that's what this trip was for, so he hadn't thought to pack that overpriced piece of plastic in his luggage. He had, however, brought some books, even though he knew he wouldn't find the time to read them. He had also made room for some dressy outfits, despite not being able to imagine any situation that would allow him to wear them. While packing, he pictured gondola rides in Venetian canals, seaside galas to attend with newly made friends, and grape-stomping excursions to a vineyard with a passionate lover who would sweep him off his wine-stained feet.

Tyler wore his Delta Diamond status proudly and for all to see. His first-class travel had been prepared by Amber. It served as another reminder that Tyler should call Jason and request her immediate escalation in the company. But not just yet—he was in no hurry to think about anything related to work. He'd add a reminder in the notes app on his phone. Later. Perhaps after a mimosa. But that mimosa—or was it two mimosas?—paired beautifully with his pre-flight Xanax, causing the voyage to slip by in a deliciously intoxicated haze. He swapped out his loafers for his travel-favorite UGG slippers. Leaving his window shade slightly open allowed just the right amount of golden light to slip in and let him slumber in his fully reclined Delta One pod.

Tyler was awakened by a stewardess named Jeannie, who tapped his should ever-so-lightly forty-five minutes before landing. He thanked Jeannie before knocking back a still-hot cappuccino. Coming slightly to his senses, he entered the lavatory with his carry-on, coiffing his hair with Kevin Murphy products and changing into his first-day-of-healing outfit. He drew heavy inspiration from *Roman Holiday*: a silk tee button down tucked into high-waisted khaki chinos, complimented by Gucci mules and a silk ascot. The outfit checked all boxes of the ideal balance: matte, sheen, and gloss. Looking in the mirror, small as it was, he felt very put together. He returned to his seat. The plane's descent into Rome was smooth. Tyler removed his AirPods and tucked them back into their case, which he kept in his Tumi cross-body purse.

"*Che bello!*" Tyler shouted to nobody in particular as he stood on the tarmac, taking in the glory of Rome Fiumicino Airport. At baggage claim, Tyler was surprised to find a stately looking gentleman in a dark, perfectly tailored suit holding a sign reading *MORGAN TYLER*. As the driver loaded Tyler's luggage into the trunk of a black sedan, Tyler thanked Amber in his mind—she always knew how to pamper him. Tyler folded himself into the back seat, and off they went.

"Sir?" asked Tyler.

"Sì?" the driver answered.

"Yes, hi. Hello. Excuse me. What is your name?"

"Yes, sir. My name is Giorgio."

"Ah! It is wonderful to meet you, Giorgio!"

"The pleasure it is mine, Mr. Tyler," said Giorgio. "Oh, no

need for formalities. *Please* call me Tyler."

"Absolutely, Mr. ... ahh... Absolutely, Tyler?"

The sedan curved its way down the veiny streets of Rome. He and Giorgio continued to chat as Tyler was swung back and forth in the back seat—Tyler suffered from that New York taxi cab habit of never using a seatbelt.

"What brings you to Rome?"

Tyler slid abruptly, involuntarily, across the backseat. Giorgio took that turn *particularly* hard. *Like a bat out of hell*, he could hear his mother saying. "A good meal!"

"Alora, you come to the right place!" said Giorgio.

The car screeched to a halt in front of an ancient-looking edifice of limestone arches and iron-gated double doors. Tyler loved it already. And it was to be his home for the next two weeks. Giorgio helped Tyler load his luggage onto the caddy that awaited the new arrival, then patted him on the back.

"Good holiday!" said Giorgio, waving farewell. A bellboy carted away the luggage while the doorman welcomed Tyler into the warmth of the lobby. Its stone walls were draped with heavily accented curtains. Tyler approached the oak-trimmed desk of the hotel clerk.

"Hello, sir. Are you checking in?" asked the unbearably sexy clerk. Tyler checked his name tag: Antonio. *Naturally.*

"Yes, I see right here. It would be my pleasure to acquaint you," said Antonio. His assertiveness caused Tyler to feel a flutter of butterflies beneath his pant line.

Antonio escorted Tyler into the elevator. Tyler could make out the musk of his cologne— Le Labo, thought Tyler. Perhaps Santal. The elevator, a relic of another era, arrived at the fifth and top floor of the hotel, its doors slowly creaking open. Antonio led the way to Room 52, removing an actual key from his pocket and inserting it into the door's actual keyhole, turning clockwise to reveal Tyler's room.

Tyler entered and was awestruck. Immaculate hardwood floors met six-inch-thick crown molding, which framed the entire room. A gorgeous white linen-draped iron-wrought bed sat in the center of the room, bookended by two night tables. At the bed's end was an oak resting lounge where Tyler placed his bags. White French doors opened to reveal a balcony overlooking the street below. Sheer curtains hung above the doors and swayed in the breeze, as if inviting Tyler to the balcony. The room looked ready for a travel magazine photo shoot. It gave off an air of impossibility—a staged set designed for a Merchant Ivory film. Tyler had, after all, instructed Amber to charge away, using his personal American Express. He took comfort in his financial security from six years of nonstop work. No, he wasn't rich. But this trip was in the realm of his budget, and that brought him much pride.

Antonio watched as Tyler walked onto the balcony. He gazed down upon the life of the city.

"I hope you enjoy your stay here, sir," said Antonio. "Please let me know if you require anything." Antonio quietly excused himself from the room, closing the door behind him. Tyler observed his surroundings. He had never been to Rome. During his junior year of college, he studied Shakespeare at the Royal Academy of Dramatic Arts in London, often traveling around Europe on weekends. He had visited Amsterdam, Berlin, Paris, and Prague, but he never made it to Italy. Standing on his balcony, he thought back to how embarrassing it was to cancel a trip to Italy because of an extended hangover. No matter. Here he was, fortunate to be able to experience the city with new eyes. The disruption of his habitual life gave him some room to breathe, and he took in the late afternoon air, the city spread out before him.

Down below, he watched as a young couple rounded the corner just past the hotel. Their hands were carefully wrapped around each other's in a way that signaled comfort and familiarity. The man said something that caused the woman to smile earnestly, looking up to him before resting her head on his shoulder. He removed his hand from hers to pull her closer under his arm. They stopped for a moment and stared at each other, oblivious to Tyler watching above. Tyler wished he could take her place, wanting so terribly to know the love she had. He couldn't make out rings on either of their fingers. A proposal would come soon, he knew it. How exciting, he thought. To have that precious security of a marriage so closely in her future stoked an envy deep within him. He left the balcony and closed the French doors.

Tyler stepped into the marbled bathroom. The sink countertop was decorated with mini bottles of Biologique Recherche serums and Diptyque travel-size perfumes. The hotel clearly knew the demographic of its clientele. Tyler turned to the claw-foot bathtub, turning its knobs so that the perfectly temperate flow was achieved. The water spilled forth from its aged pipes. He stepped in, ankle-deep, before lowering himself, almost completely submerged. A glass of cabernet sauvignon would have been perfect. Perhaps he could call Antonio for a bottle to be delivered. He trusted him to have sommelier sensibilities. Surely wine tasting was a required high school course in Italy. Antonio would see Tyler in his state of undress and be compelled to drop the costume of professionalism and join him in the bath to fool around before they made their way to the bedroom. Or maybe they could stay right there in the bathroom, their warm, wet bodies making contact with the cool, marble floor.

Tyler pulled the stopper from the tub and let the water drain to stop his fantasy from growing any more intensely. He was aware of how inappropriate the proposition would be. He grabbed a folded towel and dried himself before looking in the mirror: hairline still strong, wrinkles still at bay. He walked to the hall and selected one of the waffled robes hanging in the armoire. Comforted by its plushness, he crawled into bed and snatched his phone from the charger on the nightstand. He was experiencing that kind of loneliness born from the failure of his imagined plans to materialize. In his head, he had been whisked away by newly found friends and lovers among the cobblestoned streets, off to visit wineries, cafes, and dusty old bookshops. He unlocked his phone and scrolled over to Grindr: how terribly refreshing it was to take in the bounty of untrimmed Italian chests before him. So many American men lumped body hair—or any trace of it—into the same category as cellulite, age, and vulnerability: things to be decimated and eradicated. At least the men in New York viewed these very human attributes as such. Tyler had never dated anyone who lived anywhere but New York. When he worked in Vancouver on the streamer series, he fucked around with a casting associate on set, but it was nothing more than some playful fun after long days of shooting. In fact, Tyler couldn't call to mind the boy's name: Aaron? Anthony? He, Tyler, and Leo had all played together when Leo came to visit the set near the end of the production. Tyler didn't care enough to remember the name because before him was an entire grid of potential distractions.

He selected one headless torso and clicked on the messaging feature. He sent the signature *Hey how's it going*—devoid of any punctuation or meaning. Having always believed in casting a wide net, Tyler copied and pasted the conversation started to two other torsos of equal stature and scruff. Hoping to further entice them, Tyler selected an additional shirtless photo to send from his photo library—one that showed off everything he would like to highlight and left very little to the imagination, thanks to the speedos he wore that hugged him so tightly they'd probably be banned in many countries. His hair looked perfectly messy, sprouting into beach curls from the conditioning of the salty ocean water. His tan was even and not overdone—he had spent one summer, years ago, looking like a less-severe Tan Mom, and that was enough.

The picture was from two Julys ago, when Tyler and Leo had rented a seaside cottage in Wellfleet, on Cape Cod. The cottage had cedar shake siding and conjured images from *Grey Gardens*, which, like any good gay couple, they had seen several times. Every morning, Tyler woke before Leo to brew himself a pot of coffee. He'd walk to the porch and watch the sunrise, cresting above the Atlantic's horizon. Waves crashed and gulls cawed. Tyler could almost fool himself into believing that he was at his family's cabin on Lake Michigan, his parents soon to awake and prepare blueberry pancakes with warmed maple syrup. He was living back in those long-gone summers when a hand touched his shoulder, taking him out of his reverie. Groggy and crusty with sleep, Leo had pitter-pattered out onto the porch. He shrugged off his slumber with an overhead stretch before wrapping his arms around Tyler. They had gone to the Art House in Provincetown the night before to see Varla Jean Merman's show. On the car ride home, they laughed while trying to remember the words of Varla's raunchy parody of *School House Rock* (cock?). They'd return to the Art House that night to see *Drag Race*'s Jinkx Monsoon in her one-woman show. It was a thrill to find a venue showcasing all their favorite queens—and only a short drive away.

On the salt-washed porch, warmed by the rising sun and cooled by the sea's breeze, Tyler wished he could live in moments like these forever. He felt protected, an ocean between him and his problems. And he was there with his dear Leo. *Oh, Leo.* Where was he now? Probably with his parents in New Jersey, finding comfort in his childhood Craftsman house. He'd be drinking his father's tequila—which his father *swore* you could only get in Mexico, even though Tyler had bought it from a wholesale liquor barn on Long Island as a Father's Day gift. Leo would be playing with Benny, the family's third consecutive Bernese Mountain dog.

It was on the beach in Wellfleet that Leo had quietly snapped the picture of Tyler that was now making its way onto Grindr. Tyler had returned to their shaded set-up on the beach after swimming in the ocean. Leo told him he looked like a Bond girl rising from the ocean, pushing his wet hair back, strutting in the sand. The beach was uncrowded—it seemed like their own private getaway. Tyler joined Leo on a warm towel, dripping water on Leo's open copy of a tawdry novel to which Tyler had tried to secure the film rights—he didn't have any luck, despite wooing the author's literary agent at an all-expenses-paid dinner at Balthazar at which the agent, for an appetizer, ordered approximately seven Bloody Mary's. Leo leaned over and kissed Tyler, brushing away a patch of sand on Tyler's cheekbone. Leo kissed his hand and held it to Tyler's cheek. It was so peaceful. They had left their phones at the house, wanting to be fully present with one another.

In his hotel room, Tyler's phone lit up with a Grindr notification. He swiped it open to read that the first headless torso had replied *no americani*. Well, Tyler couldn't blame him. Giving up any immediate hopes, he got up from the bed and decided to venture down to the hotel's restaurant. He realized he was famished. Unclasping his luggage, he selected a navy blue sweater with a pair of light-washed cropped denim and some Golden Goose distressed sneakers.

Brushing out the remaining wrinkles, he stood before the hall's mirror, trying his best to avoid critique.

"Well," he said to himself. "This is as good as it's going to get."

• • •

The restaurant's host resembled Jeff Daniels in *The Hours*—cropped bangs, black turtle neck, and broad shoulders. Handsome in a matured way. He gave Tyler the up-down before collecting a menu and escorting him to the bar at the back of the dining room. Tyler pulled himself atop a backless stool and did his best to present his best posture, acutely aware of just how awkward he looked keeping his head in line with his straightened spine. In time, though, Tyler allowed himself to get comfortable, leaning forward against the bar. He rested his elbows on the granite countertop. The bartender was engrossed with a woman seated six stools down. After a long moment, he apologized to the woman and came to take Tyler's order. He stared at Tyler, wordless.

"Oh," said Tyler. "Yes. Hi. I'll just have the cabernet sauvignon. And your spaghetti, please!" Did he actually order a dish of spaghetti as his first meal in Italy? He was so embarrassed. He wondered: was there an Italian term for *faux pas*?

"Preferisci il vino rosso?" The voice came from behind Tyler. It was deep and unfamiliar. Startled, Tyler swiveled around to find a man—a *grown* man—standing before him. He was devilishly handsome in a tightly fitted button-down, slim jeans, and a pair of Converse. These were style choices few men over forty-five could pull off without signaling a midlife crisis. His facial hair was dense and trimmed closely to his face—a turn-on for Tyler. His own facial hair, the few times he grew it out, was patchy—more of a turn-off. Salt and pepper dotted the sides of the man's thick hair. Tyler was giddy with lust.

"Oh, I'm so sorry," said Tyler. "You'll have to excuse me. I'm one of those obnoxious Americans—I don't speak Italian."

The man looked around to make sure the bartender was out of earshot. He leaned into Tyler and whispered. "Don't tell anyone, but neither do I."

Tyler smiled. He removed his bag from the nearby stool—an open invitation. "May I?" the man asked.

"You may."

He winked, making Tyler's face flush out of pure excitement. Tyler's new friend took a seat, slowly and smoothly. He pushed up his sleeves as if ready to go to work.

"Is that an English accent I heard?" asked Tyler.

"London, yes. Good ear, Mr. ...?"

"Tyler. I mean—Morgan. I mean—Tyler Morgan. *That's* my name. But please, just Tyler."

"Mr. Tyler Morgan. So robust. I like it. Well, I am Mr. John Andrews. Although, I'm hardly on business, so John will do."

The bartender returned with Tyler's glass of red. Before he could inquire, John said, "I'll have whatever he ordered," giving Tyler another wink. Tyler was impressed by his coolness. He was unwavering, completely confident in the way he spoke. The English did have a sense of assurance, something most bumbling Americans lacked. Doubt plagued Americans as if it were infectious—and Tyler certainly felt he was among the infected.

They chatted through dinner, emptying their glasses, then ordering another bottle, the bartender rolling his eyes as he uncorked. They ate and drank and laughed and flirted.

"Oh my God, I ate *way* too much," said Tyler, breathing heavily. "I don't think I've had a carb since 2014."

"Welcome to Italy."

"And how did you come to be here, Mr. Andrews?"

"Well," said John, "I was traveling through southern Italy for work before stopping in Rome to visit an old friend. Then I woke up one morning and realized, why just pass through when I could stay put for a time? I found an apartment that afternoon and I've been here since."

"So spontaneous. And what work brought you to Italy in the first place?"

"I'm a paleontologist."

"But these are my bones, Diane!" said Tyler. A look of confusion flashed across John's face. "You know, Whitney Houston being interviewed by Diane Sawyer? Nothing? Anybody?"

"Oh, just wait until you hear about my nut allergy," John said, smirking. "Then you'll have your hands full of innuendoes."

"I would *love* to get my hands on your nut allergy."

Tyler was giddy about being so forward, so crude with John. He wanted John inside of him.

"And what about yourself, Mr. Morgan?"

"What about me?" said Tyler, still giggling.

"What brings you to Roma?"

"I—I just needed a change."

"How about a change right now?"

Tyler noticed that John had taken care of the check. He grabbed Tyler by the hand and pulled him out into the street.

• • •

They walked under the burning glow of old street lamps. At a corner, they turned to face each other. Before either of them could speak, they plunged into an embrace. John kissed with the confidence of a man who had nothing to prove. The kiss told Tyler there would be more—soon. It was a passion that Tyler hadn't tasted in years. He felt the electricity shooting down his body. He grabbed the back of John's neck with both hands. If John pulled away, Tyler would cease to exist—he was sure of it. He could taste the wine in John's mouth—its iron flavor caused him to fall deeper and deeper into John.

They stopped for a moment, staring at each other until they smiled, until Tyler laughed. "What is it?" said John.

"Oh, nothing," said Tyler, blushing. "I just thought of something really, really stupid."

"What is it?"

Tyler shook his head.

"Oh, now you *have* to tell me!"

Tyler took a quick breath. He knew what he was about to say was ridiculous, but the wine was loosening his tongue. He leaned into John's ear and whispered.

"Call me by your name."

John grabbed the back of Tyler's neck and pulled him so closely that they were breathing the same air.

"Okay, Tyler," said John.

Tyler pulled away, confused. John must not have understood the reference. "No, no. I said, call me by *your* name."

"I did!"

"I thought your name was John!" said Tyler.

"I go by my middle name. But my given name is Tyler. Surprise!" Tyler pulled John back in.

"So your name is *Tyler*?"

"That is correct, Tyler!"

They laughed loudly, their voices echoing down the desolate street.

. . .

Tyler awoke alone in a foreign room. He blinked rapidly, searching for clues. He looked around him. Slowly, the night before bled into his memory. Familiar artifacts surrounded him: a pizza box, an amorphous pile of clothes, two wine-stained glasses, an empty bottle of red, and a tube of—thank you, modern science—Boy Butter. Tyler looked down to find he was completely nude. He pulled the covers up to his chest. He felt like Neely O'Hara coming out of a blackout in the seedy man's hotel room in *Valley of the Dolls*. Except this wasn't seedy. And he hadn't blacked out. His mind was just a bit rusty from the wine and sleep.

On the bedside table sat a framed picture of a middle-aged woman hugging a man—Tyler! Or rather, John. It was all coming back to him. They had walked for what felt like hours back to John's apartment. He allowed himself to sink into the comforting cotton of the bed. He was at ease knowing he hadn't made a disastrous, drunken decision. No, John had been incredibly gentle—very understanding of Tyler's situation. *Oh no.* Why on earth had he talked about Leo? That kind of talk had no place in the bedroom. But John had listened. He was so sweet.

Tyler heard a faucet running on the other side of the bedroom door, which was slightly ajar. The faucet squared off. Footsteps padded softly down the hallway. The door creaked open, and John peaked in. He stood in nothing but boxer briefs, and in the morning sun, his physique was all the more impressive, especially considering he was fifteen years older than Tyler. He walked to the bed, offering Tyler a cup of black coffee.

"How'd you know?" said Tyler, accepting the porcelain cup.

"How'd I know what?"

"That I prefer my coffee black." Tyler's voice had that early morning rasp.

"I can't imagine you wanting to water down anything after seeing how you drink."

"My grandpa would always say, 'If I wanted a milkshake, I would've ordered one.'"

Tyler welcomed John back into his own bed. John wrapped

his arm around Tyler's midsection. His stomach, always a vulnerable spot, seized at the touch. He allowed his breath to slow before giving way to the touch, settling back into his body. Tyler rested his head on John's chest, snuggling into his warmth. He closed his eyes.

Tyler grew up self-conscious about his weight. At thirteen, he hadn't grown tall enough to balance out the extra pounds he put on. With puberty foreboding, the unwanted weight paralyzed him with insecurities—he was already feeling isolated because of his sudden rush of homosexual desires. He did whatever he could to fit in, feigning interest in Xbox and paintball tournaments with male classmates. During especially intense games of paintball, Tyler would remove his own paint bullets from his gun and smash them against his clothes when out of view from his teammates. The illusion of being shot removed him from the game without having to endure the pain of getting shot. What he feared the most was being outed as a fag—a new term to Tyler and one favored by his teammates. They used the word interchangeably with *idiot, stupid, fucktard, pussy,* and *noob.* Tyler tried his best to use it correctly, chastising other boys who had played poorly. It wasn't until he brought this word into his home, describing an annoying classmate, that his mother pulled him aside and told him he was *never* to use that word again under any circumstance, and if he were to, she would remove his Xbox from the console and give it away. His mom had never been so serious about reprimanding him. It troubled Tyler to see that he upset her so deeply. Beside himself with regret for using the word in front of his mother, he soon lost interest in online gaming and, as a result, soon fell out of favor with that circle of boys.

He felt so alone at that age. It was around that time when Doug, his overzealous youth group minister, delivered a sermon condemning Natasha Bedingfield's song *Unwritten.* Doug preached that the song was blasphemous: for God *had* written the future, and that in denying the divine destiny, Natasha Bedingfield was, in fact, denying God. Doug built on his thesis to say that the world had grown far too comfortable with sin—abortion, alcohol, Islamic terrorism, and homosexuality all being widely accepted. It was an ominous warning of the end times! He gesticulated wildly, sweating and shouting that to turn a blind eye to sin, the youth of America were confirming their reservation in Hell: a very real place and an even more real punishment. Thankfully, Tyler had the wherewithal to see that Doug and those in the congregation were the ones in the wrong, not him. Rather than internalizing this hatred like so many of those in the closet, Tyler found the sermons to be liberating. He saw that *they* were the blind ones, living in bubbles comforted and affirmed by the Bible Belt. They denied God by denying their fellow neighbors. If Natasha Bedingfield was a herald of the end times, then sign Tyler up to join the rest of the damned! He knew he needed to get out. But for the time being, it was a waiting game. And so he downloaded *Unwritten*, via Limewire, and chose it as his flip phone's ringtone.

His eyes drifted open to find that he was still in John's apartment.

"Oh my God," Tyler said, pulling himself up. "I fell back asleep. I'm so sorry!"

"Nothing to be sorry about."

"How long was I out?"

"Only about two hours."

"Two hours? I have to get up!" Tyler leapt out of bed, rifling furiously through the pile of clothes in the corner. He was unable to make out which pieces were his and which were John's. His breath swelled to a panic. He was *so* late! And then, in a flash, he remembered he wasn't late at all—for anything. There was no meeting. There was no pitch. There was no conference call. It was so long ago that he awakened without a list of things that had to be accomplished. Over the past few years, he worked through weekends, holidays, birthdays, and funerals, never missing a deal to be made or a film to be signed. And now he was free. This was bliss.

"Do you mind if I get back in bed?" He was aware of how ridiculous he looked, standing naked in the middle of the room, rifling through clothes, as John had watched from bed.

"I would prefer if you would."

Climbing back in, he routinely took a sip of his coffee. It was bitter, gone cold during the passing time. "Would you like me to make some fresh coffee?" John asked.

"No, no. It's fine, I swear!" Tyler grimaced. He set the cup back on its saucer on the nightstand and rolled to face John. The apartment smelled of freshly laundered linens and sandalwood. It was clean and masculine. There was so much Tyler wanted to share with John, but he restrained himself, knowing that he would look desperate and too eager to reveal himself to a stranger. But he wanted John to know! He wanted to share who he was, what he wanted and his regrets. And he wanted John to share. There was a genuine curiosity. Tyler had forgotten about the excitement of novelty. If he didn't catch himself, this rediscovery could easily overwhelm him.

John rested his head on his hand.

"What's on your itinerary today, Mr. Morgan?"

"Hopefully seeing Rome with an incredibly attractive man," said Tyler.

"And who would that man be?"

"I happen to be looking at him." Tyler inched closer to John.

"How convenient." John pulled Tyler as close as possible, almost as a dare. Tyler's face tingled from the bristles of John's beard.

"Terribly."

Tyler surrendered to the dare and leaned in to kiss John.

Chapter Four

Knowing they had only two weeks together made John all the more irresistible. It reminded Tyler of when he was young, trying to stretch out those last few weeks of summer vacation for all their worth and pushing away the inevitability of the oncoming school year. He returned less frequently to his own hotel room, spending every night at John's apartment. They fooled around, and Tyler would fall asleep easily and contentedly—better than he had in years. Before long, they even developed a routine, alternating days for making breakfast and sleeping in late. Tyler began borrowing John's sleep shirts, all dinosaur-themed and acquired by John as gag gifts or handed out at paleontology conventions around the world. Wearing the shirts made Tyler feel like the much-desired girlfriend of some middle-aged business tycoon, wandering about in the man's oversized clothing, then bringing him breakfast in bed, where he was thanked with sex. Tyler stood in the kitchen in nothing but one of those baggy shirts and a pair of briefs, soft-scrambling eggs and frying strips of pancetta. As he cooked, Tyler stared at the bookshelf in the living room.

On it were all nine of John's published books. Yes, John was unspeakably handsome. And he was kindhearted and had that alluring English accent. But what might have most impressed Tyler was John's success as an author. John's books weren't literary works for the ages—they were academic titles on dinosaurs—but he had nevertheless written *books*, and he made a respectable living from doing so. The idea of writing a book had long been a dream of Tyler's, but he didn't think of it as an actual possibility. Maybe in another life. He courted and worked with many authors and literary agents—even Alexa was a book editor—but he had never been in such intimate proximity with an actual author. And that only deepened his growing interest in John.

Tyler had never felt so free with a man, unencumbered by the demanding strictures of his job. The idea of giving his entire attention and time to another person was something he had never experienced—it struck him like a revelation. And there he was, entering his eleventh day of nothing but John, and Tyler couldn't have been happier. After finally leaving the bed and getting dressed, they found themselves walking again on the streets of Rome. Tyler, hopeless with the city's geography, took comfort in John's dependable sense of direction. It wasn't even two weeks earlier when, on the night after they met, Tyler said he needed to go back to his hotel, and John offered to walk him back. Tyler was so thankful John had done so, too afraid to come off as clingy. But John asked, and Tyler enthusiastically accepted. They talked about New York—John had just left months ago after a yearlong gig teaching at Hunter College. They spoke of missed meetings and chance encounters, Tyler shocked to learn that John had firsthand knowledge of downtown culture like China Chalet, Ty Sunderland, the Box, PrettyUgly, Frankie Sharp, and even ones in Brooklyn like the Rosemont and Three Dollar Bill. They realized they had even attended the same weekly, invite-only Drag Race viewing party at Jezebel's headquarters in Union Square—Tyler would always skip the line to go straight to his reserved seat, thanks to his friend Austin, who worked the door. Tyler and John *must* have danced near each other at some point, but fate would have it that the two locked eyes only months later, a few thousand miles away. Without realizing, they had arrived at the Trevi Fountain.

"Did you plan this?" said Tyler, howling with laughter. John played innocent with his sea-green eyes.

"Plan what?"

"Am I allowed to be a tourist?"

"Of course you are." John pulled a coin from his pocket and extended it to Tyler.

Tyler clasped the coin in his palm, noticing how cool it felt against his suddenly clammy hands. Closing his eyes, he made a wish. He opened his eyes and underhanded the coin into the fountain, feeling a sense of relief mixed with anticipation—he was thrilled to participate in this ancient ritual.

"Well?" said John, hesitantly.

"What?" asked Tyler.

"I hate to tell you this, but you're supposed to throw the coin over your shoulder."

"John, don't be ridiculous. That's only when you've spilled salt." Tyler grabbed John by the hand and they made their way back to his hotel. Little did Tyler know that he wouldn't see much more of his hotel room. Later that day, John invited him to dinner at his apartment, preceded by an aperitif. He hoped Tyler would stay the night. And that night turned into the next, then the next. After just a few days, Tyler's hotel room became a fading memory of the past, something from the pre-John times.

Tyler could no longer separate John from Rome, nor Rome from John. The two had become one, together exerting their lusty power over Tyler. His mind often made these strong associations: Washington Square Park would always be NYU, Soho would be work, the Lower East Side would always be Leo. *Leo.* Tyler had barely thought of him since entering John's world. The last time the name even left his lips was that drunken first night with John—and Tyler could barely remember what he had said about him. He felt guilt, briefly. Why had it been so easy to purge the pain of losing Leo? Maybe it had to do with leaving behind all that was comfortable—his emotional and financial security at the whim of his travels. Not that he was neglecting his emotions. No, he allowed them to come and go as he shared what was on his mind with John, who always listened. Of course, what Tyler described was entirely vague and didn't refer to Leo. John, too, had gone through a divorce a year ago, which prompted his move to New York. Even John agreed the best way to heal was to move on with life as quickly as possible. So John was more than happy to share these weeks with Tyler. And conveniently enough, Tyler needed a break from his own breakup.

Tyler felt himself gaining weight—his jeans were tighter, and his sweaters were bulging at the waist. He lied to himself: in New York, he was too scrawny and malnourished. He did his best to believe these affirmations, John confirming them every night in bed. As long as John didn't have a problem, neither would Tyler. So on they ate. There was always the phenomenal gelato place around the corner from John's apartment. They stopped by every night to see if a new flavor had debuted. Tyler's favorite was the fragola: a perfectly blended concoction of frozen straw-berries with the acidic bite of freshly squeezed lemon. They enjoyed their treats with Tyler's head rested on John's shoulder. John wore either his navy blue hoodie, on chillier nights, or a black T-shirt that rendered Tyler useless to his chest.

Unable to restrain his most basic impulses, Tyler made plans for the two of them to dine at L'Antica Pizzeria da Michele: the result of a Google search asking *what's the pizza place from eat pray love*.

"Oh my God, this is the best pizza I've ever had," said John, biting into a slice of the margherita. "How did you find out about this place?"

"Oh! Uh... Yelp!" Tyler said, too ashamed to reveal why he chose the restaurant.

"Seriously, I've been all over Yelp for months now and I haven't stumbled across this place."

"Algorithms. Can't trust 'em!" Tyler did his best to move the conversation away from his embarrassment. John paused mid-bite and stared directly behind where Tyler sat.

"My, would you look at that?"

Tyler turned around to see a framed shot of Julia Roberts sitting exactly where Tyler sat, eating the exact same pizza Tyler ate.

"Huh. Julia Roberts has been here," said Tyler as casually as possible as he turned around to finish off his slice. "You know, speaking of algorithms, the other day on Google—"

"Did you know this is where they filmed that movie? This is so cool!" John was more excited about this bit of pop culture than Tyler would have expected.

"What movie?" said Tyler. "Is that *Mystic Pizza*?"

"No, dummy. *Eat Pray Love*!"

"Hmm. That title does sound familiar. Must've been before my time."

"What gay guy comes to Italy *alone* and doesn't feel at least some tiny connection to *Eat Pray Love*?"

"I guess this one! I contain multitudes."

"Do you mind?" John asked, handing his phone to Tyler with the camera pulled up.

"You're such a tourist," Tyler said with a sigh. "But okay!"

John held up his slice, imitating the pose that Julia struck in the photo. Now realizing he would look ridiculous if he asked John for a picture, Tyler panicked. But he *had* to get his own picture with Restaurant Julia.

"Well, since we've already got the camera out, I guess you could take one of me, too." Tyler did his best to remain nonchalant.

John snapped the picture. "Who's the tourist now?" He saw through Tyler's performance.

And Tyler didn't mind. At least he got the picture.

A night rarely went by without an after-hours call for a pizza delivery. They never diverged from the margherita, Tyler unable to comprehend mozzarella that could be so fresh and soft without that rubbery pull that plagued American cheese. And the basil! You could almost smell the soil, proving that it had been plucked from its plant base just moments before the pizza was made. They'd sit at the foot of John's bed, dividing the slices evenly while flipping through the seriously dated television set that had been left behind by the previous tenant. Scanning through Italian-language programming, they would settle on some melodrama, laughing at themselves for trying to understand the most basic phrases that were quickly uttered by the actors. It was their own silly little game.

The apartment seemed to take on the couple's energy, absorbing their ever-growing comfort and familiarity with each other. Tyler's patterns and habits left their little wakes. The hand towel now sat to the right of the sink to redirect the leaky faucet. The bottle opener remained on top of the bar cart—at the ready—and no longer trapped in the utensil drawer. Little by little, Tyler's delicate touches had informed the space around them, John conforming to Tyler's preferences with little notice. So settled were they in this living arrangement that the two were shocked—hurt, in fact—when Tyler's final day in Rome arrived.

The men felt wronged, as if time had conspired against them, shortening the hours of the day to make Tyler's departure all the more sudden. The subject went unspoken throughout the day, the two going about their morning ritual of breakfast, a romp in bed, and a stroll. They talked of John's childhood that afternoon, of how he was the youngest of seven children. His parents had been devout Catholics and reproduced accordingly. Two of his siblings, Charles and Beth, had already died years earlier, John not being terribly close to either due to the disparity in age and interests. His father had been cold, never showing affection to anyone in the household. His mother was the opposite. She instilled in him what he believed to be a sense of openness and unconditional love. Tyler noticed how John's eyes grew bright and dewy at the mention of his mother, so eager to tell Tyler all the little things about her he hadn't spoken of in years, if ever. Her name was Agatha, and she was born and raised in London, the daughter of an accountant. She worked as a florist before meeting his father, leaving the store behind to raise his family. His father died when John was only eleven, leaving his mother twenty-five years of freedom. She became an avid traveler, roaming across the earth freely and without obligation, untethered to the former confines of her past life. All throughout his studies,

John would receive postcards from his mother, informing him of her latest venture. A stroke killed her when she was seventy-seven. They had spoken by phone a week before she died. John had called to tell her he had accepted a government-funded job at an excavation. She had told him how proud she was of him and that as her eighth and only unexpected child, he had been the biggest surprise and the biggest gift in her life.

Tyler and John sat together on the tufted sofa in John's living room. They rarely found themselves in there, either preoccupied in the bedroom or on one of their daily adventures. It was an unusually chilly day, and Tyler sat in an oversized sweater and a comfortable pair of jeans, having wrapped himself with a spare blanket he found on the ottoman. John leaned over to hug Tyler, resting his head on Tyler's shoulder. Tyler inhaled, comforted by John's natural sandalwood scent. Rain gently tapped against the windows of the apartment. The day seemed trapped in that twilight between late afternoon and evening.

They did their best to avoid the conversation, skating around the topic with banal discussions of the weather and which bottle of wine to open. They put on an episode of *The Morning Show*, having started the series the week before. They laughed at Reese Witherspoon's wig, tracking its unbelievable density. They agreed that she needed to give her dear friend and collaborator Nicole Kidman a call for some help in the hair department. Finally, the stalling couldn't go any longer.

Tyler spoke first.

"So, what are we going to do?

John inhaled slowly. The air felt thick, as if the apartment hadn't been dusted in months.

The smell of the rain in potted plants overwhelmed the room. "What would you like to do?"

This response gave Tyler nothing to work with. John had volleyed the question right back to him with zero indication of where he stood on the matter. For all Tyler knew, John was perfectly content with never seeing Tyler again. And that would be perfectly normal. It would be expected. John was middle-aged, and Tyler was...

not. Brief flings like these happened all the time to middle-aged people. Middle-aged people who moved on without holding on to ridiculous ideas of what could've been but what was never meant to be. But Tyler didn't operate like this. He couldn't simply let go of something that felt so passionate. So right! Being with John reminded him of the possibility he felt when he moved to New York as a pup, when he was just eighteen. John drew out that energetic, optimistic kid who had long since become jaded with age. The question lingered in the air. What would he like to do? He wanted to stay, learn Italian, purchase a villa, open a gourmet market, marry John, and adopt two girls named Sophia and Angelina. But how was he to verbalize this in a non-psychotic way? He couldn't, and so he went with what he thought was most appropriate.

Tyler spoke slowly and concisely, making sure each word accurately reflected his feelings. "I want to be very clear," he said. "I think we have something incredible here." He tried to gauge John's reaction. His face was unmoved.

"I would agree with that," said John, scientific as ever.

"But I don't want to ruin these two weeks by saying that thing you say when you really appreciate and respect and admire the person you're with," Tyler said, trying to keep his voice from wavering. "But, having *not* said that, I will say that I *do* think I might want to say those words to you soon. And if you would like to return those words to me—if you feel the same, and only if..." He noticed he was talking in circles, so he tried to cut to the point. "Okay. I'm renting this house by Lake Trasimeno for the next two weeks. And if you feel the same way, come visit me there. Anytime. And then we can go from there. Okay?" Tyler realized he hadn't been breathing.

John nodded his head. He gave no sort of indication of where he stood. "Sounds like a deal," John said, finally.

"Sounds like a deal," Tyler repeated.

"So... Let's say I do agree," John said, his eyes brightening. "How will I know where to go?"

Tyler's mouth bloomed into a smile. "I'll text you the

address!" He did his best to hide the girlish rush of adrenaline that was coursing through his body.

John leaned across the sofa and kissed Tyler. There were no tears. It didn't feel like a goodbye kiss. But it was as passionate as when the two embraced on the night they first met – the night that Tyler learned John's full name was Tyler John Andrews, the name Tyler had scribbled in cursive over and over again in the journal he had bought to document his travels—and would hide from John for fear of looking like an obsessive lunatic. If John asked, Tyler would say he was just writing down his thoughts. And in a very literal way, he was.

Tyler pulled back from the kiss to hold John's face with both hands and look at him. He made a promise to himself. This would not be the last time he would see Tyler John Andrews.

• • •

Tyler sat in his hotel room. It felt like a memory from a past life. It was time to leave Rome, and that end-of-vacation, back-to-real-life feeling was consuming him. But he wasn't back to real life. He wasn't even a third of the way through his trip. He still had two weeks left in Italy—it was just Rome that he was saying goodbye to.

Looking around, he saw that the room had been virtually untouched, save for the bed being remade by housekeeping and a towel or two being replaced. He had spent nearly four months' pay on the room—and had barely used it. But how was he to know that John would so generously open his home to him—and that Tyler would *want* to spend every night, for two weeks, at another man's home?

Rather than dwell on the subject, he took out his phone and called Alexa. It hit him that they hadn't exchanged a single text over the past two weeks. It was mid-afternoon in New York, so she'd be free. She answered.

"Hey, how's it going?" she said. "Why the fuck haven't you

answered my texts!" John—what a glorious distraction he'd been.

"Whoops! Sorry, uh, let's blame it on the time zone? But honey—it's fabulous! I wish you were here."

"I wish I were, too," said Alexa. "Too bad it's not in my budget."

"Okay, but you make more money than I do!"

"Exactly," she said. "Which makes me concerned as to how this is in *your* budget. I looked up your hotel, Tyler. What were you thinking?"

"I see this as a necessary expense. And it is totally worth it. And Alexa… I have met the most incredible man. His name is John—well, actually, it's Tyler. But he goes by John. Long story. Anyway, he's so kind and so generous, and he has been so good to me during this time. It's been perfect."

"Ah," she said. "That does sound perfect. Well, I'm happy for you!" Tyler noticed some hesitation. "And what's Rome like?"

"It's truly the most romantic place I've ever been. John took me everywhere—he's already been here for a few months."

There was silence on the other end. Tyler wanted to avoid a lecture at all costs.

"Did you spend any time with yourself?" *Here she goes*. Turning his fabulous experience into an example of how he should take better care of himself and use this time to mend his heart. But that's exactly what he had done, he thought. The last thing he wanted to do was defend his vacation to Alexa. This was classic Alexa. Tyler had known her for – God, was it *really* that long?

– eleven years. They met during Welcome Week at NYU: a garish display of feigned school spirit that forced students into unbearably awkward breakout groups to engage in ice breakers and little raffles to win T-shirts and lanyards and other various accouterments of free advertising for the institution. Incredibly bored and above it all, he and Alexa were drawn to one another during a game when they both blurted out *THE BARS!* when asked what drew them to school in the city. Laughing it off, they decided during a lulled moment to ditch the event and go barhop in the East Village for a place that wouldn't card. Finding some hookah spot on East First Street, they jumped in and decided it was worth the wasted twenty dollars on an unused hookah if it meant they could drink without question. They downed shitty margaritas while commiserating over their wasted teenage years in the vast American midwest, not-so-casually taking the smallest of un-inhaled puffs every twenty or so minutes to ward off any suspicion from the bar staff. They were both so *different.* It was almost painful to think of now, how obnoxious they had been. But they had grown over the decade: both apart and together then back apart but always coming back together.

Their friendship was woven over many pockets of the country – there were those two years when Alexa decided to move to Los Angeles and pursue her own film career before reluctantly returning to the city and her career as a book editor. He begged her not to go. He was unable to fathom a life in New York without his other half. She took his behavior personally, interpreting his sorrow as a lack of enthusiasm. Having gone a year and a half without speaking, one shitty LA breakup too many broke her down and triggered Alexa to let her guard down and finally call back Tyler. She unloaded a year's worth of silence on him, admitting that she never really belonged on the West Coast or the film business and that she would soon be forced to return to New York. He thanked her for the apology and admitted that he never meant to withhold his support and enthusiasm. In fact, he supported her so much that he always *knew* she would come back when the time was right. And so, they began again.

"Yes, Alexa. In fact, I am *very* alone right now. In my hotel room," he added, as if providing evidence in a litigation. "Of course I had time to myself. That's the purpose of this entire trip. Actually, the purpose of *this* leg of the trip was to eat, and that is exactly what has been done. And I still have two more weeks in Italy at a remote home that I've rented all for myself!"

He had talked himself into a defensive state. But she knew everything he had gone through. It should have made her happy to hear that *he* was so happy. This was the first time in years that he came to her in a good mood—a great mood, even. And yet she questioned him for not spending more time alone. How miserable that would've been, to be alone in a foreign country where he didn't know a single person. Is that what Alexa wanted? For him to mope around feeling sorry for himself, rolling around in the tarry pits of his heartache? Heaven forbid he had a bit of fun!

"Okay, Tyler! God. I just want you to take care of yourself. Okay?"

He had gone too far. He wished he could see through her frustration and recognize just how much she cared for him.

"I'm sorry," he said. "It really is good to hear your voice." He sat down on his perfectly made bed. "I really do need to pack. My train is leaving first thing in the morning."

"Okay. Travel safe. I love you."

"Love you too, doll," he said, hanging up.

Laying down on the bed, he looked up at the whirling fan above him. It almost hypnotized him, the edges of the off-white blades blurring into a uniform circle against the stark white ceiling. He was already packed, having never unpacked. He had already set his alarm. Fully dressed and too tired to pull the sheets above him, he closed his eyes and fell asleep.

• • •

He dreamt he was standing on a beach, the sandy reed up to his ankles. He heard the ocean but couldn't locate it. He turned in every direction yet failed to find the water. As he looked for any trace of it, the noise intensified. The sound of waves crashing ashore grew louder and louder until it became overwhelming. He held his hands to his ears to block out the noise as he fell to his knees. Soon, he lowered his hands, and the noise was gone. He looked to his right and there was Leo, dressed in the turquoise bathing suit he wore that summer in Wellfleet. He smiled at Tyler and pointed past Tyler. *What is it, Leo? What do you want?* Tyler looked and saw their rented house in Wellfleet. It stood alone on the sand, about one hundred yards away. *Go.*

Tyler began walking toward the house. *Go.* His walk turned to a jog as he realized he was not making any ground. *Go.* He ran and ran, muscles giving way to sinew. *Go.* The house was still impossibly far away. *Go.* The heat from the sand burned his bare feet. *Go.* He fell to his knees and let out a primal cry.

Chapter Five

The ride north to Tuscany was breathtaking. From Tyler's vinyl blue seat on the Regionale train, the passing countryside looked almost chroma-keyed. Trains had always been his preferred mode of travel. There was something so calming—and so foreign—about riding on a train. During his senior year in college, when Tyler briefly entertained the idea of acting as a profession, he came close to getting a gig at a regional theater company in Cambridge, just a few minutes away from Harvard. He would cut class to audition and catch the Acela Express out of Grand Central, making sure to hold two empty seats for himself. Reclining his seat, he'd look out at the foggy sea and watch the water come in and out of his line of vision for the four hours he was onboard. During that time, he briefly dated an emotionally needy man named Matt, who would bombard him with incessant texts. Tyler was relieved to put his phone on airplane mode during those rides and simply look out at the ever-changing scenery. It was a welcome contrast to the steamy grit of New York. The grassy pastures and stone-lined ponds gave him some space to breathe. It was only when he wasn't cast in the theater production that he came to realize how much he enjoyed those train rides.

Only half a dozen people joined Tyler in his Regionale train car. He chose an empty four-seater at the front, sliding his suitcase into the storage cabinet above him. He placed his to-go cup of black coffee on the table in front of him, watching the steam rise from its slotted mouth.

At each stop, a handful of passengers boarded the car, the spare seats filling up. He did what he could to maintain his privacy, placing totes and books across him in a sort of scattered arrangement, signaling to others that the seats might be taken. He kept his sunglasses on, averting any possible eye contact that might ask, *Is anyone sitting here?*

He unlocked his iPhone and searched for an article he had been saving for a private moment. He clicked it open and read:

Namaste, my lovelies. I'm welcoming you back to my private space of healing by opening with an energy of gratitude. I am grateful my first article moved you so much that you feel compelled to come back. I am grateful for the air I breathe. I am grateful for all you badass #spiritualwarriors out there who dare and DEFY what the world expects of us. I defied what was expected of me when I left behind my past life of being an influencer and an internet personality. I defied what was expected of me when I traded fame and wealth for life in the rural, Italian countryside. I defied what was expected of me when I DARED to find true love—and oh how it was so worth it! And it resonated with so many of you. By giving myself the opportunity and the chance to grow, I was able to connect with and inspire so many other women out there who felt stagnant in their own lives— victims of a vicious pattern of self-brutalizing abuse. We are the only thing standing in our own way, and when we finally see that, we can truly achieve anything. And that is why I am so glad to partner with a company like TIDE Detergents, who shares that same vision and goal. So, as a special treat for my readers: you can get up to 25% off all items you purchase when using the promo code SPIRITUAL DETERGENT. Now, back to my spiritual journey. I saw many comments inquiring about my relationship with the mysterious Mr. Patrick M. Yes, we are still together. Yes, he still loves me, And yes, I am still respecting his wish for privacy. However, you will have the opportunity to read more about the beautiful love we share in my upcoming memoir

EAT PRAY LOVE 2: EATING AND PRAYING AND LOVING MY WAY THROUGH LIFE. Yes, #SpiritualWarriors, I signed a book deal! It's a dream come true, and I can't wait to roll up my sleeves and do the internal work that is necessary to immortalize this quest that I've been on. I can't give too much away, but I will say that if my first article spoke to you, you should do yourself a favor and go to Amazon to pre-order the memoir, as it is guaranteed to move you and the other seekers in your life. So yes, adding "author" to the biography of Ashleigh Windham is something born from this huge leap I took! And who knows, maybe it could be yours! You just need to give yourself the permission to dive into life headfirst, ladies! Check this space frequently for more updates. XX A.W.

As Tyler swiped over to the Amazon app to pre-order the book, he felt a tap on his left shoulder.

"Excuse me."

He looked up to find three fabulously sun-glassed middle-aged women standing in the aisle before him. As he had been engrossed in the literary work of Miss Windham, he failed to notice that the car had become filled with new passengers.

"I hate to be a bother," the woman in the front said in a thick Southern accent. "But do you mind if we squeeze in here with you?" He cleared his belongings without a second thought.

"Absolutely!" he said as he pulled his coffee over to his quadrant of the table. "Do you need any help with your bags?"

"Oh good Lord, no, honey. I think we will be just fine, but thank you!"

The three women placed their bags next to his in the cabinet above before making their way into their seats. They each wore mannequin-transplanted J-Jill and Coldwater Creek outfits: culottes, breezy blouses, open-toed sandals, all in varying jewel-toned color palettes. The woman in the front chose the seat across from Tyler.

"Well," said the woman. "I'm Janna." She stuck out her hand

and shook Tyler's. He noticed how delicate her skin was, perfectly moisturized and only beginning to show its age.

"I'm Tracy," said the shorter woman seated next to Tyler. Her voice had more husk to it than he expected. She must have been a smoker.

"And I'm Angela," said the blonde woman seated diagonally opposite Tyler. She had the softest voice of the three. She was polite and demure in a way that felt familiar. A Sunday school teacher, thought Tyler.

"And rounding out our *Designing Women* quartet is me! I'm Tyler." The women happily squealed at his reference to the Eighties sitcom.

"How on earth do you know a show like that?" asked Tracy.

"It was my mom's favorite show!"

"Well, your mamma raised you right, Tyler," said Janna. "She sure did," Tyler agreed. "Now, let me guess: Arkansas?"

"Close!" said Angela, perking up from her corner seat. "Paducah. Small town in western Kentucky."

"Paducah..." Tyler said, thinking it over for a second. "The Quilting Capital of the World!" He registered the disbelief on their faces: they had found one of their own—this far from home—in the Tuscan countryside. And he was equally surprised. In New York, it was rare to run into someone from St. Louis, and even then the person would cast condescending looks at him when he confessed he was from southeastern Missouri, two and a half hours south of St. Louis. They saw the boot heel of Missouri as a cultural cesspool compared to the sparking metropolitan opulence that was their Saint Louis. And yet, there he was with three women in Italy who shared his same cultural touchstones. They reminded him of his mother's friends. These women joined Bible study groups where they would meet weekly with their nearest girlfriends over Splenda-sweetened iced tea. They hosted Pampered Chef parties in their living rooms with chocolate fountains and cream cheese-stuffed pinwheels. They made their children the center of their universe, heading up the

PTA and working the quarterly scholastic book fair. Their afternoons revolved around catching that day's episode of Oprah. They radiated warmth and comfort.

"Now, how in the world do you know about little old podunk Paducah?" asked Janna.

"I'm from Dexter, Missouri, originally. Only a hop and a skip over the Mississippi from you! When I was little, my mom and her aunts would take us shopping over there at Christmastime."

"Dexter!" Tracy shouted back. "Well, that's where my cousin Kim Milner is from!" Tyler laughed with that delight that comes from a shared connection.

"Mrs. Milner was my librarian in sixth grade!"

"Oh lord, the stories I could tell about her!" said Tracy.

"Oh, I can imagine," Tyler said. But in truth, he couldn't imagine. Kim Milner was perfectly sweet and unassuming in all the ways a middle school librarian should be. Between lectures on the importance of categorizing periodicals and hosting authors from St. Louis and Memphis, she never left much room for any personality to poke through. He remembered her in bland earth tones, always swaddled in a neutral cardigan and khaki pants.

"So what brings you three beautiful Kentucky women all the way to Italy?"

Janna reached into her Dooney & Bourke bag and produced a bottle of pinot noir. "This will be necessary."

They uncorked the bottle and divided its contents evenly among the four of them. Angela scored some disposable cups from the dining cart just one cab up. Tyler sipped his portion slowly as the women spoke.

Janna and Tracy met in fourth grade, seated next to one another in Miss Carda's class. Back then, she was just little Janna McWilliams. The two bonded over their shared love of *Laverne & Shirley*, singing the theme song together during recess. They became so inseparable that by the time fifth grade came around, they were distraught at not being assigned to the same teacher. They would meet up on the playground, commiserating about their boring classmates. Pretty soon, Tracy made friends with Michelle, who was in her class. Michelle wore thin, wire-frame glasses and came from a not-so-nice neighborhood in town, far away from the more posh—and gated neighborhoods—where Janna and Tracy lived. Having introduced Michelle to Janna during recess, the three became fast friends and formed that special bond between girls that lasts throughout adulthood. The three attended college together at Murray State, where they were introduced to Janna's roommate, Angela, who would go on to marry Janna's younger brother, Joey, only bringing the four even closer.

Every summer, the four women made a tradition of going to Janna's family's beach house in Naples, Florida. The gathering soon became a way of marking the passing years. Although the trip wasn't entirely necessary for Janna, Tracy, and Angela to stay in touch—they had all made their lives in Paducah—it was a way to get together with Michelle, who had married and moved away to Little Rock. She was living in Arkansas when she found out she was pregnant—at which point her husband walked out on her, stating that he had no intention of ever becoming a father.

Michelle gave birth with her three friends in the room and bravely made her mark as a single mother. Every summer, the women fawned over pictures of their growing children. And they collectively mourned each other's heartbreaks, swearing off men only to eventually join the dating world again. Tracy and Janna both divorced their husbands, then remarried—Janna divorcing her second husband and resigning herself to be single for the rest of her days. Despite all the tumult in their lives, they felt more stable than ever in the comfort of their sisterhood. One year, on a particularly rainy day in Florida, they went to a screening of *Under the Tuscan Sun*. After the movie, Michelle promised she'd make it to Italy one day, bringing her three friends with her to where the movie was filmed. The years passed, though, and the idea of the trip seemed out of reach.

And then Michelle was diagnosed with Stage IV breast cancer. She decided to seek treatment at MD Anderson in Houston, where her three friends joined her for the duration of her chemotherapy and radiation. At first, it appeared as if the treatment might be working. But the disease ultimately took its brutal toll on her fragile body. She passed away after six months of treatment, leaving her group of friends shattered. In the wake of their devastation, they decided to go to Italy to honor her.

Tyler sat in silence for a moment, taking in this sad account.

"I am so sorry," he said. He took a sip of his coffee, dampening the effect of the wine.

The three women sat in a way that told Tyler they hadn't spoken much about Michelle's death until that very moment. The loss was still fresh. Finally, Janna spoke.

"Thank you, baby," she said. It was so simple and sincere.

As Tyler sipped his coffee, an idea struck him. "So, the three of you are out here doing your own little *Under the Tuscan Sun* trip?"

"Yes," said Angela. "We've even booked a bus tour of the filming locations!" "They take you right up to the house where they filmed it," said Tracy.

Tyler smiled, feigning surprise. He did his best not to reveal anything.

"I see," he said. "And you're staying at a hotel in Cortona?" He threw back what remained of his wine, swallowing it in a big gulp. The three women refilled their own cups. He pushed his cup forward as Janna uncorked a second bottle.

"Yes!" said Janna, pouring from the newly opened bottle. "There's this little inn in the middle of town. You know, there's not a ton of hotels around Cortona. The main tourist attraction really is the movie."

"Huh," said Tyler, eyes cast down at his clasped hands. "Do you think the three of you would like to join me for the afternoon at the place I've rented? I'm pretty sure lunch is included, so we could all eat. I'd love to have some new friends over. And it's just up the hill from Cortona, so I could drive y'all back to your hotel after."

"That would be so lovely!" Janna said.

"Absolutely," agreed Tracy.

Tracy held her freshly topped-off cup of wine in the air, signaling the others to follow suit. They joined her in an Italian toast, trying their best to clink the cardboard rims of their cups. Misjudging the amount of force required to do so, a tiny stream of wine spilled down the side of Tyler's cup, staining the rolled sleeve of his button-down. Before he could reach into his bag, all three women produced their own Tide To-Go pens. He accepted the nearest pen and attacked the stain. He loved how maternal they were. He smiled at them. They were all archetypes of his past life. They drank together, looking out at the midday sun that warmed the scenery before them.

•   •   •

After driving up the cracked, rural pavement in a Fiat SUV rented outside the train station in Cortona, the foursome arrived at the entry gate of their destination. The gates of Villa Laura parted and widened forth to accept the Americans into her sprawling, pastoral arms. The pavement gave way to a chunky gravel driveway that was lined with olive trees. Just past the trees were countless rows of grape vines. The gravel drive wound to the right, and there sat the centuries-old estate.

The women stared open-jawed at the villa, each inhaling a sharp burst of air. The Adirondack green window panes, arched doorways, and pale yellow exterior were unmistakable.

"Tyler," Janna said, drawing out the R in his name. "Is this...?" It was as if she were too afraid of disappointment to complete the question.

He continued to play dumb. "Is this where I'm staying?" he said as casually as possible. "Yes."

"No. Is this what I *think* it is?"

Yes, it was what she thought it was. Villa Laura was the film's stand-in for Bramasole, the villa that Frances Mayes had purchased for herself on a divine whim when traveling through Tuscany. Villa Laura was *the* villa from *Under the Tuscan Sun*, and

Tyler had rented it entirely for himself. The Fiat rolled to a stop and the women eagerly threw open the doors. Tyler hopped out and joined them on the driveway.

"Tyler," said Janna. "This is unbelievably kind of you, inviting us to come see this. Especially when—" she paused as her voice broke. She gathered herself and continued. "Especially when you know what it means to us."

The four stood together, admiring the villa. It really was stunning, Tyler thought. The house was stately, as if proud to have weathered so many years in that very spot. In the outside world, just past the fortress of stone walls surrounding the property, so much had changed. But the villa itself seemed impervious to time.

"Does your hotel have a cancellation policy?" he asked.

"Tyler, you can't be—." Tyler stopped Janna.

"Janna, I have rented this ten-bedroom villa just for me. And clearly, we've all run into each other for a reason! Please. I would be honored if the three of you would stay with me. Would you like to join me?"

They looked at each other, their eyes widening.

"Yes!" all three women shouted. Leaving behind their luggage, they walked to the villa's main door, which had been propped open for them. At the entrance stood a serious, portly woman in a striped button-down and navy blue pants. Tyler shook her hand, hoping her demeanor would soften a little. It didn't.

"Mr. Morgan," she said. "Welcome to Villa Laura. My name is Giovanna, and I manage the estate." She looked at the three women before returning her gaze to Tyler. "My apologies. I was under the belief you were traveling alone."

"Oh, I was! But there has been a change of plans. I hope that's alright." He did his best to ward off any tension his new friends might experience from Giovanna's blunt manner.

"Yes, sir … that will be quite fine." She yielded enough for Tyler to feel at ease. She motioned for them to enter the home, and they obliged.

The luxury of the interior matched the elegance of the exterior. Throughout the villa were terra cotta tiles, arched passageways, cozy creme furniture, and marble countertops. Nooks were accentuated with warm pockets of countryside accouterments. Doors and windows had been opened, and a gentle breeze enlivened the place. Tyler caught the passing scent of a freshly zested lemon. The smell energized him. He watched the women move about the space, wide-eyed, as if they were parading about in someone else's dream.

"So, what do you think?" he said.

"Oh my..." said Angela.

"...*God*," finished Tracy.

There was something about their Southern politeness that Tyler adored. He knew women like this from his youth. Women who shared the same hairstylist, insisting on the same highlights and the same layered approach to their hairdos. Women who justified gossip by disguising it as prayer requests. Women who were plucked out of *Steel Magnolias* and *Fried Green Tomatoes*.

In the kitchen, a chilled bottle of limoncello awaited them, Tyler locating the source of the zesting. Giovanna instructed the young woman working in the kitchen, Anna, to serve the guests some of the liqueur. Anna obliged, and Tyler raised his glass in a toast, knocking back the citrusy, sugary drink.

The estate was comprised of three structures: the villa, the farmhouse, and the limonaia. Crafted with heavy stone and accented with bricked detailing around the windows, the villa seemed to extend, without end, toward the pool. At the pool's eastern edge lay the farmhouse: the mecca for Tyler and his friends, as this was where most of the film's shooting took place. It was decided that, as this was Tyler's trip, he would take the farmhouse for himself, and the women would take bedrooms in the villa. The villa was equipped with a full-time staff—Giovanna was merely one among many. They were available at any hour, for any request. Janna, Tracy, and Angela were beside themselves with excitement, oohing and aahing at every amenity and luxury listed by Giovanna during the tour of the grounds. The landscaping was immaculate. Perfectly manicured grass cut perpendicular to fields of wildflowers and Caradonna sage.

The four went to their respective rooms to unpack. They agreed to reconvene in an hour or so by the pool—the perfect unwinding from a day of travel. The three women made their way to the main house as Tyler turned to take in his new home for the next two weeks. The villa had undergone a tremendous overhaul after the shoot's conclusion. The owners, with a keen eye for business, saw the opportunity to take advantage of the movie's sentimental fans, flipping the property to a five-star Tuscan getaway. Despite his well-honed cynicism about the film business, Tyler fell for the lemon trees and stone pathways, as would any other tourist.

He opened the front door, noting its heaviness as he pushed his weight into the handle. It was as if he had stepped back into his childhood when he first saw the film. He was twelve years old and had just begun sixth grade. It was a particularly difficult time for him, having gained the pre-pubescent weight that made him unpopular among his athletic classmates. In sixth grade, P.E. was divided into two groups: P.E. and Advanced P.E. The sorting was decided by the fifth-grade P.E. coach, who assessed whatever potential athletic abilities an eleven-year-old might possess. Tyler had shown little to no promise by that age. He struggled with the ten-minute mile, often having to take breathers after only a quarter-mile. He would complete the mile alongside stoner goth boys and the girls who wore pajama pants to school. He was then expected to do at least fifty sit-ups within a minute. Tyler would hit half that many, if he was lucky, his soft belly contracting in sharp spasms.

It was no surprise when Tyler received his sixth-grade class schedule before the impending school year and found that he was assigned to P.E., no astounding superlative preceding the course's title. The lack of surprise didn't soften the pain as he learned that every one of his friends was awarded coveted spots in the illustrious Advanced P.E. Tyler felt destined to live forever among the unattractive, ne'er-do-well rough-housers he was forced to run track with and play against in small-team basketball scrimmages.

The dodgeball tournament was a rite of passage in Dexter Middle School lore. A cruel invention by the sixth-grade P.E. coaches, the tournament was held a month into the school year. Tyler had been dreading it since hearing of its existence in elementary school. The tournament was meant to be an exercise in school spirit and athletic potential, but it was more of a masochistic display in which Advanced P.E. students would decimate out-of-shape kids.

Tyler grew withdrawn the week of the tournament. His mother couldn't help but notice his change of mood. She feared her son might be the victim of bullying. At the time, there was a big push in the media for parents to spot early signs of bullying. Oprah highlighted tragic stories of parents who lost their secretly bullied children to suicide. After dinner, she knocked on Tyler's door and asked if she could talk with him. She asked him what was on his mind, and Tyler was so relieved. He couldn't keep secrets from his mom, but there was no way he could have ever brought himself to confess his internal conflict to her. His shame had talked him into believing he was stupid for worrying so intensely over an event that trivial. But she allowed him the breathing room required to explain his troubled mood. And so, he began speaking. He explained his worries, his fears, and his physical shortcomings, which would all be put on display for an entire class to see. She listened to him, taking note of the rise and fall of his voice as he made clear what had been eating him alive. When he finished, she hugged him and told him it was going to be okay—she promised. He wanted to believe her.

Tyler woke the next morning and entered the kitchen, where his mom waited every morning with breakfast prepared and his lunchbox packed. But that morning, she sat there at the kitchen table with no breakfast and no lunchbox in sight.

"What's going on?" asked Tyler. She was already dressed for the day. "How about we do something fun?"

He followed her to her Toyota Camry and climbed in. She pulled out of the driveway and started driving into town, passing the street that would take them to school. Instead, they headed north on Highway Sixty as she sang along to her *Cher: Greatest Hits* CD that always stayed in the car's player. It was her favorite album. After ten minutes on the highway, Tyler finally asked her what was going on. His mom never condoned truancy, let alone celebrated it. She told him that if any of his teachers were to ask, he was recovering from an asthma attack. A sudden weight was lifted from Tyler. Life flooded back into his face. She had phoned the school that morning and alerted them of his compromised condition and that he would be staying home on a strict regimen of antihistamines and Nebulizer treatments. Tyler reached over and hugged her tight, thanking her profusely for what she had done for him. She took in the rare moment of physical affection from her hormonally unstable preteen.

"I love you, Mom."

"And I love you more than you'll ever know, baby."

They arrived an hour later in Cape Girardeau, the closest thing to a city in a sixty-mile radius. Together, they went to Olive Garden—a treat usually reserved for shopping trips and doctor appointments. They feasted on the bread sticks and salads. Tyler ordered the Tour of Italy while his mom stuck with her signature tortellini. Leaving the restaurant, they walked over to the Cape West 14 Cine to see what was playing. Checking the posters out front, Tyler chose *Under the Tuscan Sun*. He liked the commercial but didn't think a movie of that prestige would ever make its way to the Dexter Twin Cinema. They ordered the extra large bucket of popcorn and two large iced Cokes. They sat in silence, eating and drinking, watching Diane Lane navigate love, life, and friendship while abroad in her new life in Italy. She reminded Tyler of his mom. Her dark brushed-back hair and even her complexion seemed to be like his mother's.

They possessed an effortless beauty that so few women in rural farmland seemed to have. After the movie, his mom said how jealous she was of the character who bought an ancient villa in Tuscany, a woman who was given a second chance at everything and soaked up the beauty that surrounded her. They both said they'd visit one day and see the house from the movie. Tyler promised her it would happen one day.

. . .

Janna, Angela, and Tracy relaxed by the pool; wine glasses filled and well within reach. Tyler saw them from the window in the upstairs hall of the farmhouse. Coming down the tiled staircase, he walked out the front door and joined them poolside.

"Here you go, honey!" said Tracy, extending a chilled white wine. Glass in hand, Tyler sat down on the spare patio chair and relaxed his lower back into the cushioned pillows. The sun was warm but not hot. He could feel his skin tanning already. He decided to forego any preventative wrinkle measures and happily accepted the UV rays. If there was wrinkling in his future, so be it. For now, he'd be gorgeously tanned by the late afternoon Italian sun.

They lay in the sunshine, silent, under no pressure to make conversation. The sun began its descent over the western pastures, causing the slightest chill. It wasn't long before Tyler drifted off into a nap. When his eyes opened, dusk had settled over his surroundings. He looked around to see the women were no longer in their patio chairs. Standing up, he spotted them through the window of the main house, enjoying the warmth of the sitting room with cups of coffee. There was something so comfortable about their friendship. It was clear that they had all experienced so much life together. Tyler tried to imagine their arguments, their reconciliations, their joys, their birthdays, their funerals, and all the small in-between moments that united them. He wondered what he would be like at their age.

Who would still be around him, putting up with his nonsense and calling him out when needed? With whom would he carry on traditions? He had never experienced the calling of fatherhood, but he had imagined himself as the fun, carefree uncle in some child's life. He could bear that responsibility. But he was an only child. And none of his friends seemed on their way to having kids. It was hard for him to imagine connecting with a child. It had been so long since he was even around one. He found it difficult to communicate with children, never finding the balance between condescending to them and being honest with them—the balance required to both bolster their confidence while relating to them. And so he avoided them, ducking around colleagues at Christmas parties and staying far away from the child stars who were cast in his projects.

Walking into the main house, he was welcomed by the rich smell of freshly brewed coffee. The windows were drawn shut to insulate the home, staving off the evening chill. A fire was going in the stone fireplace, casting a golden glow. He stood for a moment outside the door before joining them, taking in the conviviality of the scene.

"Did you enjoy your nap?" asked Janna.

"Oh, did I *ever*," Tyler said, installing himself on the spare chaise longue. "Now," he said. "I have one very important question: What's for dinner?"

• • •

That night, he dreamed again that he was in Wellfleet. This time, however, he sat inside the rented house, looking out the window at an ever-extending beach. The sandy reed grew taller, reaching up to caress the bottom of the windowsill. The cottage was empty, save for the wicker rocker where he sat. Condensation fogged the panes of the window, obscuring his view. There was an uncomfortable silence that engulfed the house. He looked down at the floor and stomped his right foot on the wide-planked wooden boards. But there was no sound. He lifted his head again to look out the window. Far in the distance, Leo sat on the sand. Tyler squinted to try to see him better. It looked as if Leo were retching. Was it food poisoning?

Tyler stood up and approached the window. The house was furnished again, the way he remembered it. Underneath the window sat the bookcase with dog-eared copies of *Rain Man* and *The Corrections*. He wiped the fog away from the window, his hands wet with the dew. No, Leo wasn't retching. He was crying. Tyler did his best to hear him, but he couldn't make out anything discernible. He banged against the windows, knowing it must be the thin layer of glass that prevented the sound from traveling. Tyler punched and punched, but the glass was impenetrable. He finally gave up, his hands red from the banging. He looked again, and Leo was only a few feet away from the window. But he wasn't wearing his turquoise swimming trunks. He was wearing Tyler's Speedo. The window fogged up again. Tyler wiped and wiped at the glass, finally able to remove the accumulated mist. He pressed his face against the window. *What?* It must be the fog. He wiped it away again. It wasn't Leo who was out there crying. It was Tyler. He woke up in a fright, his heart racing.

Chapter Six

The next morning, Tyler looked at his phone to find a leftover notification from Grindr. His eyes still blurry with sleep, he swiped open the app to find out who paid him some attention as he tossed and turned. A message read: *OMG!! Tyler Morgan!? waht the fuck r u doing in Tuscany bitch? Txt me.* Flustered, he clicked on the sender's profile. *Oh, God. Please don't let it be someone I've worked with.* The idea of having to explain his presence here to a colleague crushed his soul. His brow was dotted with sweat—he was desperate to find the identity of the messenger. The profile picture showed a seemingly tall, handsome, bearded man about Tyler's age, shirtless on a beach. The smile was so familiar, each tooth white enough to signal digital manipulation. His hair was thick and coiffed perfectly to one side, the waxed eyebrows even darker. He held an opened bottle of what looked to be Dom Perignon, condensation dripping down its side. *Oh my God.* It was Blair—Tyler's roommate from college and his former best friend. Tyler tried to remember the last time they spoke. It must have been that time they bumped into each other after graduation outside of Yankee Stadium, the two hugging before parting ways with their families. They still followed each other on Instagram—Tyler noticed that he and Joel, the boyfriend Tyler had set him up with in sophomore year, had stayed together. He was excited at the prospect of a potential reunion, and he scrolled through his contacts and called Blair's number.

"Tyler Morgan!" said that almost-forgotten yet familiar voice.

"Blair Sanders!" Tyler shouted back. "How the hell are you?"

"That's a loaded question. At the moment? Hung over. And I would hope you're the same."

Shockingly, happily, Tyler wasn't. He had paced himself with only two glasses of wine on the train, the shot of limoncello, one glass at the pool, and he barely touched the Negroni that was served before dinner. He and Blair had fended off a multitude of hangovers during their time at NYU. They seemed to never miss a party their freshman year, going out most nights and working tirelessly to secure their place in Manhattan's gay social circles. Blair also made extra cash as an escort for a higher-up at Conde Nast. Blair would've slept with him for free, he swore, but who was he to turn down the offer? Blair was from a wealthy Chicago family, so he wasn't dying for the money—it just seemed like a fun thing to do at the time. Blair would brag to Tyler about all his celebrity run-ins on dates—Anne Hathaway was just *too* much at dinner the night before—and Tyler would sit there listening, envious. Things like this never happened to Tyler—he felt like he had to beg just to get a response on a dating app. Tyler's only conquest to date had been a man he was casually sleeping with in a Barrow Street townhouse between his Tuesday morning classes. Blair was rewarded for his beauty, but Tyler had to work hard to get any recognition.

The night would begin at either Pieces or the Boiler Room—dingy gay bars on opposite sides of the Village. Well liquor cocktails were the most efficient choices on nights out. Blair and Tyler had been on a big vodka Red Bull kick, finding that the caffeine buzz helped stave off any crash brought on by the alcohol. Properly buzzed, they'd catch the Uptown A to Forty Second Street, then walk north to the Hotel Paramount. PrettyUgly was *the* Friday night party in New York that year, and Blair had taken one for the team and slept with the party's producer. That allowed Blair and Tyler to slip past the cordoned-off crowd and give their names to the doorman. Allowed entry beyond the black iron door, the two descended the spiral marbled staircase of the Diamond Horseshoe and into the bowels of Manhattan's elite drug-fueled *it* scene.

At the base of the stairs was a flickering chandelier whose placement gave the illusion that it had crashed from stories above: a Bacchanalian tableau. Everything would be in full swing by the time of their arrival. They did their obligatory hellos, kissing the cheeks of secondary friends and new acquaintances. These relationships were necessary to maintain as they secured their pending attendance at so many other similar events. It was this same group of high-powered social gays who could get Tyler into parties at the Jane, Le Bain, the Boom Boom Room, the Box, and the West Village townhouses of C-List queer celebs. Performers such as Amanda Lepore and Joey Arias would take the stage for pop-up numbers, performing burlesque stripteases and singing chanteuse staples. The crowd went wild every time.

The dance floor at PrettyUgly *was* impressive. On any given Friday night, Tyler found himself grinding next to *Somebodies*—there was the time he felt a tight hand on his waist and looked over to find a recently out and famous sitcom actor giving him a squeeze and a wink. And there was the night when Blair had taken one too many Valiums and threw up on Zac Quinto's leather boots, gingerly dancing away from the mess before getting noticed. There seemed to be an endless supply of friends handing out Adderall and molly on the dance floor. Blair and Tyler rarely checked the pills before popping them into their mouths. *Party now, think later.* That was the motto back then. The party's photographer hawked around the halls of the party, snapping photos of attendees to publish on the private Facebook page. To be selected as a subject was an honor of the highest rank, meaning one was attractive enough, fashionable enough—and fuckable enough—to be used as free marketing, luring wannabe art school kids and closeted businessmen to that line on the street above. Now, all that seemed so long ago to Tyler.

"Wait," said Tyler into his phone. "Blair, what the fuck are you doing out here? Vacay?"

"Do you have time for drinks?"

The two old friends decided to meet that night at a bar in town called Ciao Ciao. Tyler had absolutely no plans, but Blair made a point to say that he was clearing *something* to be with Tyler. It was so like him to make his friends feel like the most important thing in the world—while also making it clear that they were a burden. Tyler let it pass. Blair happened to be visiting with some friends outside of Cortona for the next week at some friend's aunt's country home—or something like that. Blair was still the master of networking vacation homes. He mentioned to Tyler on the phone that he had been on an extended stay in Florence. He couldn't believe the odds of Blair being only miles away—after years since last speaking. Tyler almost wished that he and Blair had stayed closer. Tyler traded out all of his gay friends for Leo, endowing him with the role of both lover and friend. Leo didn't have any queer friends, and never had. To Leo, Tyler's college years were dark and glamorous. To Tyler, it was something necessary and far behind him. Leo never had that experience—he was wrapped up in the tragically hetero world of the collegiate athlete. And he held it against Tyler.

As he closed the villa's green door behind him and stepped into the morning, he smiled at the glowing sunflowers in the garden before him. He felt a whirring vibration as a bumble-bee buzzed by his head on its way to the flowery feast waiting to be pollinated. He took in the pool and admired its sparkling blue splendor. Its still waters reflected the morning sun, lending an aura of calm to the villa. Tyler remembered that in *Under the Tuscan Sun*, Diane Lane's character befriended her neighbor, the xenophobic olive farmer. Tyler always wondered how she could see the good in him, trusting that he would eventually accept that his Italian daughter had fallen in love with a Polish boy. As Tyler stood there in the serenity of the villa, he, too, felt capable of seeing the good in anyone. He entered the main house and followed the smell of breakfast to the kitchen. The women were gathered around the oval, pastel table in the nook, finishing breakfast.

"Hello, girls! How's your morning?"

"Wonderful! I'm fuller than a tick at a dog show," said Tracy as she polished off a cornetto.

"We saved you some," said Janna. She patted the empty seat next to her, already pulled out. Tyler joined them and admired the full plate. Scrambled eggs, sourdough toast lightly buttered, a scoop of ricotta drizzled in olive oil, two pieces of slab cut bacon, and an assortment of ripened fruits complemented by a steaming cup of coffee.

"This looks phenomenal," he said, tearing through a bite of toast. "What are you three up to today?" He sipped his coffee. It was divine. He scooped a dollop of ricotta, carefully spreading it onto the toast.

"Absolutely nothing," said Janna. "Apart from sitting by the pool and waiting to see what the day would bring."

"Sounds fabulous to me," said Tyler. "I might run into town later just to look around. Oh! And you'll never believe this. My college roommate is in the area. You'd think he was *stalking* me. We're going to meet up for drinks tonight."

"Wow, that *is* unbelievable!" Angela said. "It's almost as if this is exactly where you're supposed to be."

•　•　•

The center of Cortona reminded Tyler a bit of a rural version of Silver Lake in Los Angeles. Community-oriented, familial, and placed ever so inconveniently on the inhospitable landscape of a mountainside. Tyler and Janna walked past farmers shepherding goats, venders selling fresh produce of every variety, and handsome men loading crates of wine into the opened cellars beneath the storefronts. Tracy and Angela stayed back at the pool to nurse their jet lag, so Tyler and Janna hopped in the rental car and drove back down the cracked road to see the real Cortona for themselves. Tyler and Blair weren't meeting until nine that night, so he had plenty of time to see the ins and outs of the village.

As they walked, they passed a girl walking hand in hand with her mother. The mother held a wicker basket filled with bright red tomatoes, and the girl skipped in time with her mother's steps while humming a tune. Tyler watched as she hopped over a puddle, the mother pausing to wait for her daughter. As Tyler came upon them, he smiled and nodded his head, allowing the girl to pass. He turned back to Janna.

"How old are your kids?"

"Thirty and twenty-eight," she said. "*Lord*," she added, letting out a big sigh.

"They're on both sides of me!"

"You're only twenty-nine?" asked Janna. Tyler stopped in his tracks.

"*Only?* What would you have guessed?"

She clearly didn't interpret her usage of "only" as a microaggression. "Honestly? Thirty-five? Thirty-six?"

He thought his heart skipped a beat. He imagined his hair graying on the spot.

"Oh my God," he said quietly. "My time is running out."

"Oh, heavens! Honey, no, no, no. I didn't mean because of your appearance! Lord, I'm well past caring about that. That didn't even cross my mind. You look great! It's just that—you just really seem to have it all together. I mean, how many movies did you say you already produced?"

"Six," he said. "And a TV show."

"See? That's unbelievable, Tyler. Really. And all before thirty. I feel like my kids are just getting started. I'm still paying for my daughter's rent, for heaven's sake! I told her that it *ends* at thirty. If I had half a mind, I would just cut her off now. But I know she wouldn't talk to me ever again. And my son makes pretty good money working at our family's bank, but lord, he needs my help for *everything*. He's almost thirty-one, and that boy is *still* on the tit! Sometimes I wonder if maybe I babied them too much, maybe I should've made them be a little more independent. But every time they came home with a problem, my door was open and I would help them fix whatever it was. I said I was going to be the parent I wish I had growing up. I was hell-bent on doing the exact opposite of what my parents had done. I knew they loved me, but I don't remember them ever making it a point to tell me. All my friends' parents were the same way. The parents of the sixties and seventies, they were social. They loved their friends, and they loved their parties. But the kids seemed to be last on their agenda. And all my friends are in the same boat as me now. We did everything we were supposed to. We showed up for the pizza parties, we never missed a soccer game, we missed meetings to pick them up from school early when they got sick—we did everything right. And now my kids can't even apply for an apartment without needing my signature. Your parents must be incredible."

"They were," he said, knowing it was easier to agree than elaborate further on why that wasn't entirely the truth. As they passed a boutique, Janna stopped and looked into its window.

"Oh, this place looks fabulous! I'm gonna duck in."

"No problem! I'm going to walk down the block and see what's around. Meet you here in five or ten?"

"Sounds perfect," she said, walking into the store.

Tyler continued down the street, checking out each storefront as he passed. He came upon a bookshop and peered in. Stacks of Italian-language books cluttered the shop. Purchasing one would be a cute memento, sure, but he still had India and Bali ahead of him. He'd need to keep his luggage light. As he gazed past the bookshelves, he nearly gasped. Standing behind the counter was one of the most gorgeous men he'd ever seen. He was tall, tanned, and with a full head of neck-length hair. For all Tyler knew, this man could have been Timothée Chalamet's body double. He froze. Had the man just winked at Tyler? Or had it been a cruel trick of the imagination? He pulled away from the window, flustered. He felt embarrassed and quickly proceeded to the shops ahead of him.

Tyler sometimes found it hard to tell when someone was flirting with him. Maybe it had to do with a lack of self-esteem. Maybe he was unable to take things at face value. Before Leo, he had gone on a string of unsuccessful dates with attractive, successful men. His placement on the Thirty Under Thirty (at twenty-five, no less) opened up a new world of eligible bachelors just begging to know him. But the dates always ended with Tyler too unsure of himself to make any moves, not wanting to come off as pushy. This led to awkward hugs and exchanges of unsatisfying goodbyes. And there was always talk of second dates that never came to fruition.

Even Tyler's first date with Leo wasn't supposed to be anything special, as evidenced by the lack of enthusiasm that went into planning it. A week prior, the two matched on Tinder, where Tyler was drawn immediately to the pictures of Leo swimming in some sort of NCAA-sanctioned event—Tyler tried and tried but could not deny his internalized desire to be with the all-star athlete. They had a charming rapport, exchanging quips about Wendy Williams's latest debacle and Katy Perry's recent embarrassing appearance on *The Ellen Show* when Leo went silent. Never one to take ghosting well, Tyler called him out the next day, to which Leo responded with aloof humor. The two decided they would meet the following night for drinks at The Belfry – a charming, relatively-hetero establishment on Fourteenth Street – for the convenience that it was directly across the street from Leo's apartment, a request at which Leo was oddly adamant. A sign of good times to come?

It was an unusually chilly September night. Tyler clacked up Third Avenue in his snakeskin Chelsea boots and Opening Ceremony bomber. He was running about fifteen minutes behind. He gossiped into his cell phone on the trek with a college friend about another ex-college friend's recent embarrassing turn as a viral internet sensation making cringe-worthy videos of herself pointing out the obvious differences between New Yorkers and Californians – perhaps the best use of her BFA in Drama. They gasped and giggled about their second-hand embarrassment (and unspoken jealousy) of the whole whirlwind as he arrived at the bar. He looked around but saw no trace of the swimmer in the pictures. He texted a quick *SO sorry! Just got here!*

Only to receive back *hey so sorry running behind, b there in 5.* It was so rude! How dare this finance bro be late when Tyler himself was already running late! And what did Leo have that was so important? Some merger, probably. Tyler didn't even know what a merger was! Tyler could promise that whatever had tied Leo up wasn't half as demanding as the *least* challenging aspect of Tyler's work day. Whatever, he would try his best not to let this get in the way of the date. He centered himself and reminded himself that he was interesting enough to carry the conversation.

Tyler had just finished producing his second feature film *Sleepwalkers* – a moving drama about a trans woman finding her way home – and had never felt more self important. Having been single for over two years from his first and only serious relationship, he was ready for an actual boyfriend again. He had grown lonely in those early years of his career. He wanted someone to share his dreams with, share his accomplishments. And to have those dreams, those accomplishments received and appreciated. He had two years of getting the fun out of his system – hooking up with random, wealthy men at The Boom Boom Room, having his drinks paid for and a few drugs offered. At twenty-five, he could no longer get away with that kind of twinkish behavior.

And then across the street walked Leo, standing about two inches taller than Tyler – an astoundingly attractive quality as it wasn't too tall that it pulled an awkward focus to the difference but just enough to make Tyler feel smaller without feeling tiny. Tyler stuck out his hand to introduce himself and immediately retracted, noting how awkwardly formal and straight the introduction was. Leo laughed and stuck out his hand as he smirked at Tyler's faux pas. Tyler liked that. A man with a sense of humor, how perfect! How rare! There were so many joyless people in New York, all too serious and self-obsessed. Hellbent on curating some Instagrammable facade that they carried into their personal lives. It was nice to laugh at himself.

The pair took one look inside the unusually populated Belfry to find it uncomfortably stuffed with bodies.

"Wanna find another bar?" asked Tyler.

"Sure!"

They walked East on Fourteenth, looking for somewhere more accommodating.

A few blocks East, they passed the sparsely attended Crocodile Lounge. Tyler had never been, but it came with the highest praise from Alexa who claimed that for every drink purchased, a free pizza was included. The thought alone had bloated Tyler, but that night the idea didn't seem so terrible. It seemed kitschy and adorable in the way that many first dates are romanticized but fail in execution. They gave each other a shrug and walked inside.

The multitude of empty drinks and poked-at pizza soon came to resemble Jesus feeding five thousand – enough to go around for the entire bar. They giggled over Ryan Murphy's successes and missteps and Jamie Lee Curtis's tweets while inching closer and closer to one another. Tyler stared into Leo's eyes, unable to make out their color in the dimness of the bar. Whatever they were, they made Tyler melt and unable to look away. Without noticing, Leo had subtly placed his hand on Tyler's thigh. What a nice move, he thought. Leo said it was so impressive that Tyler was a film producer, this adoration only intensifying Tyler's rising attraction.

"Can we go some place a little... gayer?" Tyler finally asked.

"Absolutely."

The two clumsily stumbled their way to Phoenix, an East Village staple known for its karaoke nights hosted by drag queens such as Tammy Spenx and Terra Hyman. Nuzzled in the back corner of the bar all alone, Leo looked at Tyler.

"Is it cool if I kiss you?" asked Leo.

"I actually thought you'd never ask."

Leo fell into Tyler. Tyler placed his hands on Leo's chest, made broad from a lifetime in the water. Tyler fingered the top button on Leo's shirt until it popped open. He was relieved to find gorgeously thick chest hair. They continued to kiss as Tyler traced the outline of Leo's nipple under the shirt. Tyler hadn't been kissed – or kissed – like that in so long. He hadn't allowed himself to ever truly kiss a hook up – it pushed the encounters into a landscape he wasn't entirely comfortable with. But on that night, he didn't hold himself back. He felt that undercurrent of passion and desire under every taste. They almost gasped for air as all energy was focused on wholly feeling and experiencing the other. It was magnetic. It was hopeful. It was hot!

As the bartender yelled out for final call, they collected themselves– soberly broken away from the protected privacy of their own little world.

"If I weren't proper, I'd ask you to accompany me home," said Tyler, wiping away the moisture from the corner of his lips.

"Ah, totally," said Leo.

"So... I guess I'm not very proper."

And so, Leo walked with Tyler back to his apartment.

. . .

After passing a quaint cafe and the village's post office, Tyler found himself at the street's end. His little journey was complete. *Okay*, he thought. *I'll just walk back and see if he's still standing there. If he notices.* Retracing his steps, he noticed the bookshop's door had been propped open. He quickly glanced in and saw him: he was standing behind the counter. And he was smiling. Tyler stopped and held his gaze, remembering to smile back. The man waved at Tyler slyly. Tyler felt his shoulders tense and stepped inside. He was taken aback by how sacred the space felt. Wooden planked floors met ancient stone walls. Row after row of oiled oak shelves held leather-bound books. A cat slept at the foot of the desk, its chest gently rising and falling with each breath.

"*Benvenuto*," said the shopkeeper.

"*Benvenuto* to you too!" Tyler said, blushing, embarrassed that he was welcoming the bookseller to his own store. He shut up before he could ramble any more. The man laughed at Tyler. But it wasn't a condescending laugh. His gentle smile told Tyler that he was just teasing.

"I love your shop!" Tyler said.

"You love my father's shop. But I will tell him of your approval." There was that wink again.

"I'm Tyler."

"I'm Andrea."

Of course he was. As if Tyler needed any more *Call Me By Your Name* allusions on this leg of the trip. He had at least half a decade on Andrea, if not more. Tyler rarely found himself attracted to younger men. But in *this* case, he could make an exception. He was trapped in that mentality of the college-aged, recently-moved-to-the-city twink. He was unable—or rather, unwilling—to accept his aging status. But at least he was aware of it! This phenomena seemed to plague so many of his gay contemporaries who clung onto vestiges of today's youth as if they were rats holding on to a floating piece of furniture off a sinking ship.

They downloaded apps like TikTok and embarrassed themselves as they danced shirtless to top ten hits, further emboldened by the tragically horny people who praised them in the comments. They wore cropped shirts with ironic logos such as the United States Post Office or Chili's. Their footwear of choice was an all-white high-top Converse sneaker accentuated with mid-calf-length tube socks. They took ketamine and went to Olivia Rodrigo concerts, making the actually age-appropriate fans and their parents deeply uncomfortable.

Their knowledge of queer history began and ended with *Drag Race*. Bonus points for citing their one trans friend! But the one trans friend was never actually a friend, just someone they met maybe once. Or followed on Instagram. They virtue signaled in their social media bios, copying and pasting info graphs without even reading the content first. Unprompted, they took to Twitter to defend themselves in nuance-less threads, claiming that queer people were robbed of an expressive, honest youth. So not only were they allowed to act so immaturely and irresponsibly throughout their twenties and thirties in an exercise of finding their true selves, it was their right! Tyler never could get behind this argument. It lacked any sort of accountability for one's life and the choices that brought about and enabled that life. How could they whine so frequently about being unable to find a meaningful relationship when every choice they made negated and obstructed the possibility? They wanted to sound deep and in touch with themselves. They came off as desperate and inappropriate.

"I assume you're here on holiday?" Andrea asked.

"Yes, for the next two weeks! And then I'm off."

"Oh? Off to where?"

"India!" Tyler said. "And then Bali."

"Italy, India, and Bali?"

"Oh my!"

Andrea laughed. Referential humor *could* transcend borders. But Tyler was suddenly reminded of the question that *Legally Blonde* posed: was this man gay or simply European? Unsure of the answer, he decided it was best to leave. He didn't want to force anything that might not be there.

"Well, thank you for your time," said Tyler. "I'll come back soon and bring my friends! They would love this place."

"Oh? What are they doing now?"

"They're at the little place we've rented. Probably in the pool! Speaking of, are there any lakes or rivers around here to swim in? I've heard the water here is beautiful, and it's my last chance to see any open bodies of water until I get to Bali. Except for the Ganges. The holiest water on earth, they say. But probably also the most toxic. So maybe you could show me a place around here sometime?"

"Absolutely. It would be great to see you again," said Andrea, winking yet again.

. . .

The taxi went far too quickly. He was hoping he'd have more time to mentally prepare for the exhausting exercise of reuniting with a former friend. Tyler was trying to come up with topics of conversation when the taxi lurched into the gravel parking lot of Ciao Ciao. The driver had been playing Joan Baez's live album *From Every Stage*. Tyler recognized it immediately. He had discovered it on Valentine's Day, four years earlier, when he and Leo rented a cabin in West Saugerties, just outside of Woodstock. Tyler had picked out the record from the cabin's extensive vinyl collection. They cooked grilled cheeses using freshly baked sourdough and smoked gouda that they had bought at a small grocery in town. The scratches of the record's needle filled the home with a nostalgic sound. Snow blanketed the woods outside, sealing Tyler and Leo into their own cozy pocket of the Catskills. By the time the album reached Joan's cover of Bob Dylan's *Forever Young*, the two were undressed and entangled with each other on the floor. They slept in the lofted bed that overlooked the living room and out the window where the moonlight sparkled on the untouched snow.

Tyler felt grown up. It was the first time he had vacationed with a boyfriend. The idea of spending the night in a new town with a partner had always seemed so out of reach. It was an experience reserved for the grownups in his life—older cousins, aunts, and uncles. He and Leo stayed awake talking through the night. They were desperate to hold on to the day before it could slip away. In the morning, they were wrapped so tightly around each other that Tyler could hardly longer discern whose limb was whose.

The driver's choice of music made it difficult for Tyler to focus on meeting his old friend. He exited the cab, fiddling with his clothes as a way of stalling. Finally, he entered Ciao Ciao, filled with thin, attractive couples at high-top tables. He looked around for Blair. Nothing. He pulled out his phone and texted *here!* At the bar, he ordered a gin and tonic, not feeling bold enough to pick out specialty cocktails from the menu. Phantom vibrations buzzed in his pocket. He checked his phone every eight seconds or so—*had he missed a text from Blair*? He sat at a corner booth, sipping his drink. He felt a tap on his shoulder.

Tyler let out a shout. "Oh my God!"

There he was: practically unchanged. Tyler jumped up and hugged his old friend. Blair still stood about seven inches taller than Tyler—all the more easy for him to steal attention.

"It is *so* good to see you, you fucking bitch!" He pecked Tyler on the cheek. Tyler gestured toward the open seat.

"Here, please, sit! Let's order you something."

"Oh, don't sweat it," said Blair. "I've had quite the head start today. I'll let you catch up." Blair's drinking habits had always teetered between *good-time-party-girl* and *why-don't-you-come-to-a-meeting-sometime*. Blair once got so drunk at a brunch that he missed his mother's birthday. She and Blair's family had come all the way from Chicago to celebrate in New York since Blair had been unable to fly home due to "finals." Tyler saved his friend's hide that time by telling his mother that her son was experiencing a horrific bout of stomach flu.

Tyler stared at Blair in the dim light of the Tuscan bar. His style had stayed the same. He played it safe, rarely straying from the basics. He loved a slim pant, a bomber jacket, and a black tee. His budget had clearly upgraded, though. On his wrist was that Cartier bracelet everyone seemed to be wearing. And it was not the Fulton Street version. The waiter appeared, and Tyler put in an order for a second gin and tonic. Blair ordered a vodka rocks.

"Okay, wait," said Tyler. "Why the actual fuck are you in Tuscany?"

"Well, I have the same question for you!"

"Okay, my answer is rather simple. I want to hear you first!"

The waiter returned with their drinks, setting them carefully on their coffee table. Its Marilyn Monroe coasters reminded Tyler of the celebrity-covered ones under the always-flowing

Mezcal Mules at the Blond in New York. Countless Tuesday nights when they danced under the disco glitter of the rotating mirror ball before stumbling out for some potato skins at Remedy Diner. He and Blair had shared so much.

Blair knocked back his vodka as if he were parched after a run. Not even a wince. He set the empty glass back down on the coaster.

"Well," said Blair. "I suppose you can add *Divorcee* to my resume now. How glamorous is that!"

"Excuse me? I wasn't even aware that you got married! Sure, très chic in a *Valley of the Dolls* way, but *what*? Please explain!"

It was during their sophomore year at NYU when Tyler had his first serious boyfriend.

He remembered how jealous Blair was. So he decided to help him out. He introduced Blair to Joel, a business major Tyler had met through a friend of a friend. He was everything Blair was looking for: assertive, hot, and, most important, loaded. He came from a prominent Connecticut family and had a guaranteed career paved for him upon graduation. Blair and Joel hit it off. Blair morphed into the boyfriend Joel wanted: quiet and passive. Arm candy. He didn't mind sacrificing himself—it was entirely worth it. As their relationship got more serious, Tyler and Blair started to drift apart. The year was coming to a close, and Tyler and Blair no longer found it necessary to be roommates. They each found their own off-campus living arrangements for junior year and silently parted.

Blair left that summer to study abroad, in Paris. He and Joel decided they would stay together despite the distance. It was only two months, it was nothing. Only twenty years old, and seduced by life in France, Blair soon found himself embroiled in an affair with a fellow student. It was nothing serious, but when he got back to the States, Blair was sick with guilt. He couldn't lose Joel—the promise of a stable financial future with him was too important. But he felt he needed to tell Joel. And so he did. He told him that it was meaningless, that the sex was subpar.

That he would never see the boy again, and that it was over.

Joel disappeared for a few days. No calls, no texts—nothing. And then he reappeared at Blair's apartment, ready to discuss what Joel had confessed. He said he was prepared to move forward. But he began making rules for Blair to follow: Curfews, hourly check-ins, permission to make plans. And Blair complied. Then came the resentment. Every one of Blair's moves was questioned. Who had he been with? What had they done? Who was on that call? It went on for years. And then, two years ago, Joel proposed, and Blair said yes. They were married at Joel's family estate in Amagansett, in the Hamptons. All went beautifully for a year and a half. They moved into a townhouse in Chelsea, adopting a golden doodle named Pucky. Blair had done it. He had achieved what he always dreamed his life should be.

And then, six months ago, Blair returned home from grabbing a cup of coffee and bringing the mail up to the apartment. He began opening it absentmindedly, tossing aside credit offers and other useless envelopes. He tore open a letter, then saw it was addressed to *Mr. Joel Foster*. He tossed it onto the kitchen island, leaving it there for Joel when he got home. Blair then went about his day: SoulCycle, lunch with a friend, shopping at Neiman's. When he got home, Joel was sitting there at the island—sobbing. He quickly began apologizing, begging for forgiveness. He told Blair everything. That he had cheated during the entirety of their relationship. He confessed to countless nights at the Cock and sucking off men weekly. He confessed to flirting with baristas, then fucking them after their shifts ended. There were days when he lined up three, maybe four men in a row off of Grindr, traveling from one apartment to the next. And he had done it all unprotected. Which led him to the opened mail on the kitchen island that he *assumed* Blair had read: his STD screening. Gonorrhea: positive. Chlamydia: positive. Syphilis: positive. And yes, HIV: positive.

Blair stood, dazed. He watched his husband weep.

"Joel. I didn't even read that. I opened it accidentally and left it there for you." Blair watched as Joel screamed out in pain. Pain of his own making. Blair had been put through an emotional hell by a man who had done so much worse than he ever could have. He understood, though. Joel was projecting. He was projecting all of his self-hatred onto Blair.

"But ... but are you okay?" Tyler asked. "I mean, are you healthy?"

Amazingly, he was. Sure, Blair tested positive for gonorrhea, chlamydia, and syphilis. But what homosexual hadn't! After a strict regimen of antibiotics (which nearly destroyed his GI tract), he was easily cured. But for all those years with Joel, he never stopped taking PrEP. He was never sure why. All his other married friends had long gone off the drug, except for those in open relationships. But something in him, some voice, had always poked at him, nudging him to keep taking those pills. So he had. He tested negative for HIV and filed for divorce.

"I'm so sorry," said Tyler. "I can't believe what you've gone through." He stared at his second gin and tonic, drained. Blair, meantime, had gone through two vodka rocks as he recounted his failed marriage. So much for letting Tyler catch up. "But wait," he continued. "I still don't know why you're in Italy!"

"Oh!" said Blair, cheery as ever. "I'm here with some friends who offered to fly me out to distract me from my divorce. My friend Kitty has a house in Florence, so I've been up there. I leave in two days."

"Wow," Tyler said. He wasn't sure what else to say to Blair. The ease with which he bounced back, all chipper, was worrying.

They flagged down the waiter and placed a third round of drinks, both feeling rather sober. Tyler saw what looked like glee in Blair's eyes. Was he proud of his victimhood? Or was it the label of being divorced? Did he feel entitled to so much more life—the good and the bad—than Tyler? He felt as if he was being pitied. Only Blair could make him feel like the person worthy of pity in this story. And Blair hadn't even said a word.

"So, what's your reason for being here?" Blair asked. The

waiter returned with their drinks.

"Oh. Well, do you want the truth? Or do you want the PR version I've been telling people here?" He felt the effect of the third gin and tonic, finally.

"Is that even a question? Give me the whole truth, nothing but the truth, so help me, God!"

"Amen! So ... my boyfriend of four years dumped me—"

"I heard," Blair interrupted.

"You heard? What? How?" Tyler took a swig of his drink.

"What do you mean *how*? You're a pretty important player in the NYC fag scene, babe. And you're every bartender's favorite Oscar-nominated patron! Word gets around, doll."

Tyler was stunned. He hadn't even considered his personal life to be gossipy fodder for the queens of the city. He didn't want to show how distraught this made him.

"Oh. Okay. So you also know that I quit—"

"Quit your job? Yes, your breakdown, or to quote Miss Kelly Killoren Bensimon, your *breakthrough* has made it through the grapevine. But the quitting and this trip are because of the breakup? Huh. I assumed it was—"

"It was what?" asked Tyler.

"Oh, you know... I had heard what happened to... Oh. You know what? I'm gonna run to the bathroom real fast." Blair stood, uneasily, and looked around for the bathroom. "I'm just glad you're getting out of New York a bit. It really is necessary. Now. Where's the bathroom?"

Tyler pointed him in the right direction, and Blair excused himself from the booth. Left by himself, he wondered: What was Blair implying? That a breakup wasn't reason enough for a much-needed vacation? What a hypocrite! Blair was there for the exact same reason. But he said he had heard something else. What were his exact words? *What happened to...* To what! One of his failed movies? What was it that Blair knew? Some huge plot that made Tyler the laughing stock of the town? Was it that the myth of his career had grown bigger than what it actually was, causing others to think that he was pitiful, hopeless, even *entertaining*? Had pursuing what he thought would make him important actually made him laughably *un*important—to the point where old friends felt he needed to escape his career and life in New York?

Or was what Blair implied more insidious than what Tyler imagined? There was no way Blair could've meant *that*. How would he have even heard? And besides, Tyler didn't need any more time to deal with it. It had left him practically unfazed. He had done what was required, and now he was fine. No, he decided, it was simply out of the question for Blair to have implied *that*. It would've been completely inappropriate and out of turn.

Blair returned to the table in a fluster. He flung himself back onto his seat, grabbing Tyler by the arm.

"Oh! My! God!"

"What? What just happened?" Tyler assumed Blair had run into a celebrity in the bathroom who needed to get away from it all in Tuscany—maybe Geena Davis or Daryl Hannah? Someone worthy of queening out over.

"Okay. So. There's this stupidly hot guy at the urinal next to me who was *fully* giving me the up-down. So. At the sinks, he's just *staring* at me, practically begging to hook up. So I reached over and grabbed his ass—"

"Blair! You can't just grab people in a bathroom! Without permission!"

"Oh my God, we are *fags*! That's what we're supposed to do! That's like half the fun of being gay—we get to have stupid, fun sex like that whenever we want. And I deserve it, given all I've been through! *Anyways*. He gets cold feet all of a sudden, pushes me into the wall and storms out. What in the actual fuck?"

Tyler was astounded. Had Blair always been this entitled? That he would grab a stranger's ass in a *straight* bar—in another country!—and then take offense when it didn't go as he expected? Blair felt he was owed attention, that it was his birthright. His height alone drew attention anytime he entered a space, and that brought him immense pleasure. When Tyler and Blair had entered a room, Tyler conceded all hope of landing any eligible man. Things hadn't changed.

Blair raised his arm and snapped his fingers to get the waiter's attention. Before Tyler could say anything, Blair had ordered them another round, telling the waiter to make it as quickly as possible.

"Maybe you should drink some water, Blair," said Tyler, pushing his still-full third gin and tonic to the side, away from Blair's rolling gaze. "And maybe some dinner! I could order something. What're you hungry for?"

"Oh, fuck off!" Blair shouted. "I don't need any fucking *water*, Tyler. You think I'm that fucking drunk? Don't you fucking patronize me, Tyler Morgan."

It was as if a switch had flipped. The person who returned from the bathroom was not the same person who had left the table moments before. Blair was prone to these little irrational outbursts during their friendship, but it was always the result of a coke binge—usually in the early hours of the morning after long nights out. Clearly, that wasn't the case tonight. But then Tyler looked at Blair—truly looked. His mouth curled inward rapidly between words. He chewed his lips as if they were bubblegum. His knee shook nonstop, stomping the ball of his foot to the tiled floor. His eyes were dilated, and they were darting everywhere. It couldn't have been clearer. He had snorted some rails in the bathroom. Even his right nostril—always the right nostril, Tyler remembered—was red around the edges.

The waiter brought them their drinks. Tyler watched as Blair downed half his glass in a gulp. He gasped for air as he finished, wiping away the vodka at the corner of his mouth. Tyler pretended to drink his fourth gin and tonic, trying his best to ward off any unwarranted aggression. He didn't want Blair to feel like he needed to hide it. He could see the secrecy was causing him great anxiety. He knew it was best to just get it out there.

"Not to get all Lisa Rinna on you, but were you doing coke in the bathroom?" Tyler asked. Blair's leg briefly stopped shaking as he continued to chip away at his fingernail. His head bobbed yes before he spoke.

"Yeah. Yeah, I was. You want some?"

Before Tyler could answer, Blair produced his signature little dime bag of white powder. Tyler went through all of college having seen the actual stuff only a handful of times after Blair left his life. His close friends far preferred margaritas and marijuana. Once he fell out of the incestuously tight circle of Manhattan elite gays during his sophomore year, Tyler managed to avoid the hardcore drug scene that had plagued so many of his peers.

"You know what," said Tyler. "That's super nice of you, but I've gotta get up early, so I don't want to mess around with my circadian rhythm tonight. But thanks!"

"You're so fucking lame," Blair snarled. The blood vessels beneath his skin had caused his face to redden.

"Um. What're you even talking about?"

"You never want to have any fucking fun, do you? God, you're such a fucking loser. You could never keep up—even back then! Whatever. It's so fucking stupid. It's not worth it."

"No, it's not worth it! You're insulting me because I'm turning down some shitty bar coke on a Tuesday night? Get a fucking grip, Blair."

"No wonder your fucking boyfriend dumped you! You're a motherfucking loser! You're single as fuck with *nothing* to show for it! I at least am getting a goddamned apartment out of it! You're so fucking jealous, it's sad." Blair laughed as he ranted. He swung his arm out as he gesticulated, knocking both their drinks to the floor. The glass shattered as it met the hard tile, covering their feet in glass and liquor. The bartender's attention turned to them, now concerned about the shouting that had escalated into shattering. The bartender quickly came over.

"Is everything alright?" he asked.

"Yes, sorry, it's just a—"

"No, everything's not alright," Blair slurred, interrupting Tyler. "This motherfucker here wants to try and fucking call me a fucking addict or something, and—"

"Sir, we need you to leave," the bartender told Blair. He gestured toward the door.

"Are you fucking kidding me? This fucking bitch right here starts a fight with me, and you want to kick *me* out?"

"Sir, please, we are asking you to leave," he said again. The bartender had about an inch and fifty pounds on Blair. He flexed his crossed arms as he stood, unmoved. Blair took one look at him and made up his mind. He stood up, refusing to look toward Tyler, who sat there, shocked at how quickly everything escalated.

"Hey," Blair shouted at Tyler. "I will fucking *ruin* you when you get back to New York. Fuck. You." He spat the words with acid. They burned right through Tyler. Blair turned back to the bartender: "You will be losing my business *forever!*" Blair pulled out his phone as he stumbled toward the door, unable to push it open. The bartender finally pulled it open for him and ushered him out. Tyler could see Blair screaming into his cell phone before rounding the corner, finally out of view.

Tyler sat for a moment, unthinking. He was shaken by the volatility of what just occurred. Tyler had forgotten how many times in the past Blair had had one too many (and snorted one too many) and quickly turned on those around him. It was frightening. But Tyler knew it had nothing to do with him, not truly. He was neither the cause nor the cure.

"Are you okay?" asked a familiar voice. Tyler looked behind him to see the man from the bookshop—Andrea!

"Oh my God. Andrea! Yes... Thank you. I'm okay. Just a bit rattled from the yelling and... everything. I'm sorry—it's embarrassing." He felt the entire bar watching him. He, the abused friend, the one left behind.

"Good. Are you friends with him?"

"Am I friends with him? No. At one time, yes. But years ago."

"Oh, good," said Andrea. "He is trouble. I walked into the bathroom and caught him snorting something. He offered some to me before trying to kiss me. I asked him to stop so I could wash my hands, but I was backed into the wall. I had to push him off so I could leave."

"Oh God. I'm so sorry," Tyler said.

"It's alright, but thank you. I'm glad you're not with him. You are too good of company for someone like him." Andrea smiled at Tyler as he placed his hand on his shoulder.

"Hey, do you mind if I leave you my number? It'd be great to see you again before I leave. If not, I totally get it."

"That would be wonderful," said Andrea. He handed Tyler his opened phone, and Tyler texted himself from it. He stood up to face Andrea.

"I am meeting some friends, but I will reach out," Andrea said.

"Awesome. I'll be waiting."

Andrea turned to exit the bar. Tyler was left standing there in the wreckage of Blair's divorce. He looked down at the splintered shards and the gin that soaked the leg of his pants. As Andrea reached the door, he turned around to say, "I'll call you."

Chapter Seven

Ten days passed, and Andrea hadn't called. Tyler kept his phone near him at all times, waiting for it to buzz. He feared that if he were to step away for a moment, Andrea would clandestinely call, and Tyler would miss his chance. He sat awake in bed, waiting for the sun to rise. He rolled to his side, looking out the opened windows. The sun was daring to rise over the horizon of trees. It crested the olive trees and spilled golden light through their leaves. The time had come to face another day.

• • •

He held each woman's hand as they stepped into the boat, helping balance them as the vessel rocked back and forth. First was Janna, who accepted Tyler's help without thought. Next was Angela, who tried her best to step from the dock to the boat by herself before collapsing into Tyler's extended arms. Last was Tracy who, despite the relative safety of their short excursion, already wore her neon orange life vest. Tyler grabbed the cooler stuffed with chilled wines and the snacks wrapped in parchment paper by Giovanna.

That morning, they had made the twenty-mile drive down to the still waters of Lake Trasimeno. Though it lacked the sapphire blue of the Amalfi Coast, on a foggy day at Lake Trasimeno, it was impossible to see shore to shore, which gave one the illusion of being at sea. And it was an easy drive from Villa Laura.

Janna and Angela were seated at the stern as Tracy sat in the boat's middle aisle. Tyler assumed his position at the bow, the boat's sole rower.

Fifty yards out from the shore, Tyler paused rowing. He reached under his seat and retrieved the chilled bottle of pinot grigio from the cooler. He uncorked it and poured four glasses, distributing them among his fellow passengers. Giovanna had been careful enough to package the glasses in newspaper to prevent any from breaking. They toasted as the boat swayed ever so gently in the lake. Only a handful of other boats dotted the lake that day. After sipping half his glass, Tyler placed his wine on the seat next to him and began rowing again.

"Tyler, we can take over for a bit if you'd like to relax," said Tracy.

"We really don't mind!" Angela said, between sips of her pinot.

Tyler nodded to their wine glasses. "I have a feeling that if left to the two of you, we'd still be in the marina." Tracy and Angela giggled and toasted to that, their glasses sparkling in the midday sun.

"I can't believe we have to leave tomorrow," said Janna.

"I know," said Tyler. "It's not fair! You're leaving me all alone at the house for two days."

"Well, honey, it would've been fourteen days alone at the house if we hadn't met!"

"I actually cannot imagine what these two weeks would have been like without you. Thank you all *so* much for spending this time with me. It really does mean the world. I feel like I've had three extra moms on vacation with me!"

"Honey, we thank *you*!" Janna said. "You've given us the trip of a lifetime." Tracy and Angela nodded in agreement.

Tyler continued to row east, and the boat made good progress, given that he was the only person rowing.

"Where'd you learn to row like that?" asked Tracy.

"He's a farm boy! That's his Southeast Missouri showing!" Angela said.

"They don't have bodies of water in Dexter!" Tracy said. "Unless you count the duck hunting ponds."

"We spent a few weeks every summer up on Lake Michigan. I'd take little kayaks and canoes out on the lake and do one-man productions of *On Golden Pond*."

Tracy spewed white wine across the boat, and the women cackled. "You *have* to be joking," said Janna, gasping for air.

Tracy stopped laughing as she squinted into the distance. She brought her hand to her brow, shielding the sun's intensity to get a better view. "What is *that*?" she asked, her eyes trained on the horizon. Tyler looked to see a speedboat cruising in their direction. It was advancing at a good clip.

"Oh my God!" Angela screamed. "Row!" Janna yelled.

Tyler dug in as quickly as possible. His tricep muscles plunged down, sinking the oars into the suddenly thick water. He panted as he repeated the motion to avoid the oncoming catastrophe. The boat was about a hundred yards away, steadily approaching. He rowed faster. His forearms were beginning to cramp. The women screamed as Tyler rowed, the speedboat sprinting closer and closer. They waved and shouted in its direction, trying to catch the captain's attention. At about fifty feet away, the captain looked up from whatever was distracting him to finally see the rowboat. He hooked a hard left, nearly capsizing his own vessel. The violent turn sent a big wake in their direction. It crashed against the side of the boat. Tyler, still paddling furiously—and obliviously—was tossed overboard.

He opened his eyes to find that he was underwater. It happened so quickly that he hadn't processed it. Shards of light and shadow shot around his body as he held his breath. He looked up and swam to the surface. Breaking the surface, he began to panic. He had no life vest to help him stay afloat. His body metabolized the adrenaline far too quickly. He was exhausted. He smashed his arms down at the water, desperate to keep himself from drowning. The women leaned to the starboard side to help him. But the sudden shift in weight distribution created a dangerous imbalance. As they reached to grab Tyler's pleading hand, the rowboat capsized, plunging all three into the lake. Tracy, having worn her life vest, floated effortlessly at the lake's crest and swam back to the boat. She heaved at the capsized craft, trying to flip it over. Tyler, Janna, and Angela were at the mercy of their own swimming abilities, screaming for help. Over the shouting, Tracy heard a voice. She pulled herself as best she could atop the boat. She scanned the horizon for help. Who was shouting at them? As she sat on the vessel, she saw a dock about twenty yards away. They were closer to help than they realized. She saw a man standing at the edge of the dock, yelling.

"What?" she cried out. She couldn't hear him over the commotion. He yelled again.

Nothing.

"Y'all," she pleaded. "There's help! Be quiet for one second!"

The three souls calmed themselves briefly enough to hear: "Just stand up!"

"What do you mean?" Tracy called back.

"Just! Stand! Up!"

Their panic paused. Tyler stopped flailing and extended his legs. They met the mossy bottom of the lake. He pushed into the earth and arose, finding that the water they were in was about only four feet deep. Janna and Angela did the same. They had managed to capsize on a sandbar within walking distance of the marina. They looked at each other, feeling a combination of shame and glee. They weren't sure whether to cry or laugh.

• • •

The incident had left them exhausted—even if they were never in any real danger of drowning. They returned to the villa and collapsed onto their beds. Tyler awoke from his nap, his eyes slowly opening. He walked to the bathroom and turned on the shower—dried algae and crusty sand were still stuck to his body. Stepping onto the stone floor to dry himself, he caught his reflection in the mirror and noticed how dark his tan had become.

How many years had it been since he had spent this much time outside? Back in his room, he threw on a black T-shirt and some linen trousers. After slipping into his white sneakers, he walked downstairs to the living room.

"Hi, honey. I hope you don't mind that I let myself in." It was Janna. She was on the sofa, freshly showered. The late afternoon sun cast a warm glow around her. She could have been Diane Lane, living out her own little movie.

"Don't be silly," he said. "It's fine." He joined her on the couch. "So, what's our plan for dinner tonight? Should we have Giovanna prepare us something special for your last night? Oh! Maybe we could ask her to fix that branzino we bought at the market the other day."

"Well, that's what I wanted to talk to you about. Remember our friend Michelle? Today would've been her sixtieth birthday. So, me and the girls were planning on having a special dinner in town to honor and celebrate her. You're more than welcome to join us."

"Oh my goodness, of course you three should be together for that. I would never want to intrude!"

"You wouldn't be intruding! I just didn't want you to think we were ungrateful guests who didn't even bother inviting you."

"I would *never* think that. And I'm so sorry that she's not here to celebrate."

"Oh, honey. Yes, it is sad," she said. "But we're exactly where she wants us to be. We're here for *her*. I can feel her with us." She looked at him. "When someone you love passes on, you don't lose them. You lose their laugh and their voice and the *person*. But they also stay with you. And when I need her most? When I feel like I truly *need* to speak with her, she visits me. In my dreams. And we talk—just like we used to."

Janna reminded Tyler so much of his own mother. She wrapped him in that maternal, unconditional comfort.

"I don't mean to sound all hokey-pokey Southern Baptist on you," she said, "but I know that God sent you into my life on this trip, Tyler. You have brought myself and my two best friends a gift that we'll forever cherish."

He had to turn away. It was too much to look at her. "What is it?" she asked.

"I... I just—." He collected himself. "I feel the same way. I really do. And I feel like right now, speaking with you, I feel like I'm speaking with my mom again."

"Honey," she wrapped her arms around him, bringing him closer for a hug. "Whatever the situation is between you and your momma, just know: it's never too late. This is coming from a momma herself. I can promise you that you two can find a way forward." He sunk his head into her arms, allowing himself to be held. And for a moment, he allowed himself to believe her.

• • •

He found a DVD of *My Best Friend's Wedding* in his bedroom and popped it into the entertainment console. The women were at their memorial dinner and he had the place to himself. Why not lie in bed, swaddled in a cotton robe, a bottle of pinot noir by his side? As Julia Roberts met a fresh-faced Cameron Diaz, his phone lit up with a text from a foreign number. He threw off the layers of quilts and duvets and lunged for his phone at the edge of the bed. He swiped it open to read *ciao this is Andrea are you free tonight.* Before he could think, his fingers typed *yes! what's the plan?* and hit send. His heart raced as he awaited the arrival of those three glorious dots that showed he was typing. He yelped as his phone buzzed to life with a call from the same number. He took a deep breath and answered.

"Hey, this is Tyler!"

"Ciao!"

"Ciao! What's up?"

"Are you down for something fun?"

"Absolutely," said Tyler.

"Perfect. Text me your address. I'll be there soon." Andrea hung up. Tyler texted him the address. Andrea responded: *see you in 20 minutes.*

Fuck. Twenty minutes! He sprinted to the bathroom and took stock of himself in the vanity's mirror: this would require triage. He squirted a pump of the Kevin Murphy Motion Lotion into his hand and raked it through the coarse tufts of his hair, trying his best to massage it into some semblance of style. His face was red and splotchy from his GlamGlow face mask. He dabbed some concealer onto the problem areas, using his finger to blend it into the skin. There was simply not enough time to use the beauty blender! He vigorously scrubbed his teeth as he plugged the blow dryer into the European socket, blasting the heat onto his mangled curls. Hightailing it to the closet, he grabbed a salmon Acne hoodie and some distressed jeans. He wanted to keep up with Andrea's effortless style—this man, after all, had the advantages of being young and, damn him, European.

The landline in the bedroom rang. He ran from the closet and snatched it from the receiver.

"Hello!"

"Hello, Mr. Morgan," said Giovanna. "You have a visitor at the gate. Shall I allow him to enter?"

Motherfucker! How had Andrea managed to get to the house so quickly?

"Yes," he said. "Please let him in!" He slammed down the phone and went to the mirror. He looked perfectly okay, he thought. Thankfully, it was nighttime, which was far more forgiving than daylight. He walked downstairs to the entryway and opened the door. Andrea stood there in the driveway, propped against an aqua Vespa.

"Oh, hello!" said Tyler as he admired his ride for the night. "Just call me Lizzie McGuire!"

• • •

Tyler wrapped his arms tight around Andrea's sturdy core as the scooter soared down the winding roads of the Tuscan hillside. The midsummer air whipped at their faces. He rested his chin on Andrea's shoulder, comforted by its steadiness.

They passed pastures recently baled for hay. The road was lined with ancient farm houses built of cracked stone lined with green moss and ivy. Tyler saw a cottage, a single light on in a window, tucked into a wooded hillside. He recognized the road as the one that led to Lake Trasimeno, in which Tyler had been flailing about only hours earlier. They turned onto a sandy path obscured by the thick of trees. Andrea puttered along, rolling over fallen logs and thorny patches. They passed a partially opened gate, Andrea ignoring the do not enter signs, and there was the lake. They were in a secluded cove. Andrea kicked the brake down and threw his helmet to the ground. He pulled off his shirt and tossed it atop the helmet.

"Uh... what's going on?" Tyler asked, still straddling the Vespa.

"You said you wanted to find a place to swim!" Andrea unbuckled his belt. He whipped it from his jeans and threw it in the direction of his other belongings. Before Tyler could reply, Andrea's jeans were unbuttoned and down to his ankles. Tyler turned away as Andrea's boxers dropped to the sand. He so desperately yearned to look but didn't wish to make Andrea uncomfortable. Tyler kept his vision trained on the trees behind the scooter as he heard splashing. Andrea was already in the lake, swimming.

"Well, are you coming?" he said.

"Don't have to ask me twice!" Tyler removed his clothes. His bare feet sent a chill up his spine as they squished into the cold mush of the sand. He tried to cover himself with his hands as he was entirely exposed by the moonlight. The icy chill of the water bit his ankles. He dunked down and paddled to where Andrea was, bathed in the black and blue of the midnight water. He looked up at the sky as he waded, taking in the infinite stars that hung above them. Andrea swam to him, his gaze also fixed on the sky.

In their pocket of the lake, no lights from the village were visible. Nor were any boats. A quiet settled above the water like a layer of unseen fog. It felt as if Tyler and Andrea existed alone in this still space. Nothing else existed beyond the lake, beyond them.

• • •

When Andrea and Tyler got back to the house, the women still hadn't returned from their dinner. Taking advantage of their absence, Tyler took Andrea to the sprawling sitting room of the main house. He built a fire, and the two of them got comfortable in a chaise, wrapped in each other's warmth. They watched the flames, the logs now crackling, and Andrea rested his head on Tyler's chest. Tyler held it tightly under his right arm. And then the silence was broken: the landline in the main house rang out. Tyler begrudgingly lifted himself up and crossed the room to answer.

"This Is Tyler."

"Mr. Morgan," said Giovanna. "There is someone ringing the bell at the gate to be opened. Should I—?"

"Oh, yes. I ordered some delivery. Please send them up to the main house." It was Andrea's idea to order a pizza—they were both hungry after their swim. Tyler waited a moment for the delivery person to travel up the driveway before he got to the door. At the light knock, Tyler swung open the door.

"Oh! Uh, hi there!"

It was John. He was holding a bouquet of yellow roses. He greeted Tyler with a suffocating hug, letting himself into the foyer. It was a long trip from Rome, he explained. Tyler froze, not knowing what to do. He felt his face drain of color as he panicked.

"It is so good to see you," John said.

"Is that the pizza?" It was Andrea's voice from around the corner.

John peered into the sitting room, where he saw Andrea relaxing on the chaise. His gaze returned to Tyler, still frozen.

"Oh God," John said. "You said to come anytime. I should've known to..." He walked to the front door.

Tyler rushed forward, blocking his exit. "John, John! Let me explain—"

John interrupted. "You know what? I'm just gonna catch the train back to Rome. I'm sorry to have bothered you."

Tyler reached for his shoulders, but John pulled away from his touch as if Tyler were poisonous.

"John, baby. This isn't what it looks like!"

"This is exactly what it looks like. I'm sorry to have accepted your invitation. Goodbye, Tyler." And with that, John brushed past Tyler and walked out the still-open door. Shaking with shock, Tyler stood in the foyer, looking out as John walked back down the driveway, calling his taxi to return. He turned around to see Andrea standing there, arms crossed.

"Oh, God. You heard that, didn't you? He's just—"

"*This isn't what it looks like?*" Andrea asked, simmering with anger. "Then what is *this?*"

"Andrea, I can explain. He's a friend from—"

"He's clearly someone in your life who should've prevented you from accepting a date with me. This is why I don't get involved with older men. Too much baggage."

"Older? Wait! That's not fair! I'm only a few years—"

"Just be quiet, Tyler. I'm going home." Andrea walked out the opened door, putting his helmet back on and kicking off the brake of his Vespa. The gravel spat behind him as he rode off, tailing John's cab.

Tyler stood alone. He was trapped in the empty villa, an ornamental, inescapable dollhouse. He brought his hands to his face and allowed the tension in his chest to finally explode.

"Mother*fucker!*"

· · ·

Tyler barely slept that night. Tossing about, sometime after midnight, he heard a car crunching along the gravel, its headlights casting shadows on the walls. He heard his friends gently exit their vehicle, making sure to quietly close the door so as not to disturb their host. Tyler cursed himself in the dark:

if only he had gone into town with the women—everything would have been fine.

. . .

The following morning finally arrived. Tyler waved to his friends as they looked back at him from the taxi. They had said their goodbyes in the foyer, hugging, then hugging once more before breaking away for good. There were promises of a reunion one day, maybe in New York at Christmastime. They made him promise to let them know when he was next in Missouri, but he told them not to get their hopes up.

He stood in the foyer as he watched their car travel down the driveway the four of them had come up only twelve days before. He was confronted with a threatening silence. He could hear the wind pushing the sheer curtains, now billowing gently across the floor. It was hard to believe his time in Italy was coming to a close—and what a depressing turn it had taken. His friends were gone, and his two romantic prospects had walked out on him in the most embarrassing way possible. The back of his throat began to ache, tightening in preparation for a sob. It was a feeling he most associated with his mother leaving for work in the mornings when he was still too young for kindergarten. His grandfather would come over for breakfast as she packed her thermos of coffee before leaving to teach fourth grade. Tyler stood at the front window, watching his mother step into her white Camry, looking back to wave at him. His throat clenched and the heaving sobs would follow as he banged his tiny, closed fists on the window in a desperate attempt to get her to return.

Tyler opened up Grindr for the first time in days. He scrolled and scrolled, left numb by the sea of torsos that filled the screen before him. He finally settled on a profile who had responded a little too eagerly to his introduction. He sent him the address to the villa, and the afternoon passed by just a little faster.

• • •

It was his final dinner in Italy and he had no one to share it with. He extended an invitation to Giovanna, who accepted with total ambivalence. They sat across from one another at the impossibly long dining table, the chatter of their silverware echoing throughout the vacant halls of the house. Tyler pushed the noodles around his plate, lacking any real appetite. Not that Giovanna noticed—she managed to eat without making any discernible eye contact. Tyler felt the awkwardness crush down upon the room. He couldn't focus on anything except for what was not being said. He felt compelled to speak.

"How's your meal?"

"I made it," she said, her eyes still on the plate in front of her. Okay. He tried again. "How long have you worked here?"

"Many years."

"Got it."

Resigned and defeated, he took a bite of the bolognese. It was delicious, but in his current state, it didn't give him any enjoyment. He wondered if he'd feel the same if he had been chewing styrofoam. He scooped another portion of the bolognese into his mouth. It was warm. He chewed and swallowed, doing what he could to ignore the silence.

"My father, he worked here."

He looked up to find Giovanna looking back at him. He put his fork back down on the plate.

"Oh," he said, unsure of what else he could contribute.

"He was the gardener. I would stay here with him when I was little. This house was so exciting to me. It always seemed impossible to me for someone to have such beautiful things. I began to work here, with him, when I was fifteen. It was only one family that lived here. The home where you have stayed. The family, they had many, many friends. And they would come to us and stay here. And one family, they had a son. He was the most handsome man I had ever seen. He was American. At the end of his family's time here, he invited me to join him in New York. And so I did. I told nobody. Not my father, not my mother, no one. When I got there, it was not what I had expected. He was not what I had expected. The noise was awful. The *smell* was awful. I cried each night, wanting to return here so badly. He was not the kind man I thought him to be. I went to work as a housekeeper in a hotel. It was the only skill I knew. And I worked and worked and worked until I could afford a plane ticket back to Italy. And I came home. It was the only place—this place—that could fix what he had broken."

She picked up her fork and resumed eating. Tyler stared for a moment. He wanted so terribly to say something meaningful to her, to let her know that he heard her, that he understood.

"Well," he said, "I love New York!"

He looked away, too embarrassed to maintain eye contact.

"Is it your home?" she asked.

"Is what?" He looked back at her, at a loss.

"Is New York your home?"

He thought for a moment. It had been a home for the past decade. So many memories were there. But did he yearn for it the way one was supposed to yearn for home? It would be a lie to say yes. He had never considered that it wasn't his home, yet when faced with the question, he simply couldn't commit to an answer.

"I..." He tried to find the words. "I'm not sure."

"Where is your home?"

She continued to stare at him as he sat there squirming.

"I don't know."

Chapter Eight

Namaste, my Spiritual Warriors! I hope that you are allowing the Light to work in each and every one of your lives. I know I sure am having trouble to keep in the Light as the pressures of the real world grow heavier by the day. But just like the girl boss anthem by Miss Spears says, "I am stronger than yesterday!" YES. WE. ARE. (P.S. #FREEBRITNEY, BITCHES!) And to carry the light just a little farther, I've got a very special treat for my readers—the first chapter of my memoir! Yes, my Spiritual Warriors, you are about to read the very opening of my story!

Shoutout to my AWESOME publisher for allowing me to show you some of what I've been working on. And remember, this is JUST the beginning. Make sure after finishing, you make your way to Amazon and hit the pre-order button (linked below) because the first eight-hundred pre-orders WILL receive a very special video message from yours truly. Without any further ado, here is the first chapter of EAT PRAY LOVE 2: EATING AND PRAYING AND LOVING MY WAY THROUGH LIFE...

"CHAPTER ONE: STRESS FRACTURE

'I traded fame for love / without a second thought / it all became a silly game / some things cannot be bought,'
—Madonna, Substitute for Love (1997)

The one question people would always ask me is, 'What is it like to be you?' A seemingly benign question, yes. The allure of the Internet celebrity is the accessibility of the whole sham. It is incredibly possible to become internet famous, for it happens every day. It is incredibly possible to interact with an internet celebrity, for we frequently lurk in the comments section of our content. And it is incredibly possible for it to all be ripped from underneath you. I would know, for it happened to me. My life has been shattered into two sections: the before and the after. The before was a long, static expanse of shallow nothingness, devoid of any depth or nuance. The before was merely the impersonation of a life. The before was the performance of self. The before was not me. That morning so many months ago is where it all began: when I woke up to the news that I had been canceled. The experience of being canceled is a particularly lonely experience—you are left with nobody and your fans and supporters have vanished overnight. But the experience of being canceled is even more lonely when the entire world is watching through the lenses of their phones. An artificial audience. And even with that thin, glassy layer of protection, nothing can protect you from the searing blaze of their judgment. My career was one of an influencer. It was my job to put myself in the public's view, accepting all that came with it, both the good and the bad. But what I could never have expected was to be torn apart so viciously, so violently, for merely existing. For no reason, the vitriol of the internet decided to set its sights on me that day, and all that I had built was torn down as collateral when I fell from where I had stood. And so, I did the only thing I knew to do: run. I ran as far as I could. And in the running, I began to find some truth. I began to experience the answers to the questions I had—"

Ladies and gentlemen, the captain has turned on the fasten seat belt sign. Please return your trays to their upright position. The flight crew will prepare the plane for landing. Thank you.

Tyler closed his phone after bookmarking the page, making sure to finish reading later. He slept for most of the journey, only waking up after being jostled awake by a bit of turbulence. He looked out his window to be greeted by a wall of gray. He slipped his AirPods back in and clicked onto the article, so eager to read the latest on Ashleigh Windham's auspicious memoir.

As the plane descended at Dehradun Airport, in Uttarakhand, India, Tyler took a deep breath, doing his best to let go of his experience of Italy. India would be a new chapter in his journey, and he didn't want to carry any residual pain into this experience. He dressed comfortably in white linens—what he believed to be the perfect outfit to check into a remote ashram. His oiled leather Birkenstocks had never been worn. He felt the unbroken leather wear into the soft sides of his feet. Thank God he didn't have to walk to the ashram, he thought.

When the plane's wheels made contact with the tarmac, Tyler clicked off of airplane mode and checked his texts. His phone dinged with an alert. Opening the message, he read, "Hope you have a beautiful and safe trip ... PRAYing for you LOL"—followed by the praying hands emoji. It was from Janna, in a group message with Tracy and Angela. He sent back "Thank you!!!" with a heart emoji. He closed out of his phone and smiled. It was so nice to be thought of. They had returned to Kentucky and resumed their lives. Tyler was curious what that sensation must be like. To have an entire life and to put it on pause for a short trip. To exist in a reality parallel to the one that had been actively chosen and cultivated. Tyler didn't so much pause his life as douse it in gasoline and toss a lit match onto it. His job was gone. His relationship was dead. And he hadn't spoken to his one friend in weeks. More than ever, he felt affirmed in his decision to take this trip.

His bus to the ashram wasn't scheduled to arrive for another thirty minutes. Standing under the tin roof of the open-air baggage claim, he called Alexa's number. The phone rang six times before going to her voicemail. He waited for the beep.

"Hey, girl! I have *so* much to tell you. Italy was truly such a cleansing experience for me. I met the most incredible men *and* women. Truly! I'll have to tell you more when you call me back—which, I guess, will be in a month? The ashram doesn't allow technology. And don't worry, I've already sussed it out online. It's definitely my most PC option. There's, like, little to no appropriation for white people to be here doing this, so we're all good. I will not be wearing a bindi, nor will I be wrapped in a saree. I'll be at the Phool Chatti Ashram, in case there's an emergency or something. I'm pretty sure there's a front desk you can call. I am going to be practicing yoga and meditation in their purest forms for *thirty* days! This is truly what I need right now. Okay—I'm pretty sure your voicemail is gonna cut me off any second now. Love you, baby! Hope you're good. Bye!"

After gathering his luggage from the conveyor belt, he stood outside in a small crowd of people awaiting taxis and rides from loved ones in modest sedans.

"Are you going to Phool Chatti as well?"

Tyler turned around to see the exact type of person he had expected to meet at the ashram. The woman was probably in her late sixties and gorgeously aged. Her gray hair spiraled into healthy curls long past her shoulders. She wore an off-white, long-sleeved shirt tucked into an ankle-length, beige canvas skirt. She carried a patched-fabric tote adorned in peace signs and embroidered flowers. Tyler could just imagine the essential oils and copies of Judith Butler essays she carried in that bag. She wore those strapped, water-proof sandal-shoe hybrids that allowed one to move in and out of creeks and knee-deep ponds with ease. She looked as if she taught elementary music class or graduate-level gender studies.

"Was it the linens that gave it away?" he asked.

"Well, that," she said, "and the fact that you're standing at the sign where the emailed instructions told us to wait."

"I'm Tyler."

She bowed her head in a greeting.

"My name is Tabitha." Tyler tried his best to bow in return—it came out as a half-assed nod.

"What brings you to the ashram?" he asked.

"Oh, I've been to many throughout northern India. But this one has come to me highly recommended by a colleague."

"What do you do?"

"I teach gender studies at Sarah Lawrence." Aha.

"Have you ever practiced at an ashram before?" she asked.

"This would be my first!"

"Ah, how glorious. I almost envy that. I think this will be a really beautiful experience for you. I didn't start practicing until I was in my forties."

Tyler noticed the callouses on her fingertips. She played the guitar. His mother had those same callouses. She would play him all sorts of songs on any stringed instrument. The guitar, the dulcimer, the autoharp. It calmed him to see those callouses on someone else's fingers.

The canopied bus arrived at the sign in a cloud of black exhaust. A bald, middle-aged man in a stained shirt hopped out and threw their luggage onto the stowaway cart. Tabitha gave Tyler a look.

"Well," she said, "I guess this is our ride!"

She forged up the stairs and found an open seat behind the driver. She gave Tyler a little wink as he pulled himself up the stairs. He passed her and they exchanged nods. Tyler walked a few rows back and found two empty seats. Without a warning, the bus roared back to life and floored ahead.

The road to the ashram was steep and rural. They passed few other cars as the bus grunted and screeched around corner after corner. Every ten or so minutes, the bus would stop at unmarked posts and a few people would gather their belongings and exit. The road ran parallel to a river, and Tyler realized it must be the Ganges. Its blue-gray rapids rushed past as the bus continued its ascent. If he concentrated hard enough, he could hear its flow over the roar of the bus's engine. He suddenly felt blessed. Here he was next to one of the world's most sacred and holy bodies of water. He watched it rush, hoping to attain some sort of divine insight just from its proximity.

After about twenty minutes, only Tyler and Tabitha remained on the bus. She turned around and gave him a little wave. As the bus crested another hill, the driver veered right and pulled into a nestled community of white buildings tucked into the side of the mountain just beyond a gate. The driver jumped up to gather their luggage. Not so gently, he tossed them onto the ground to be picked up by their owners. Tyler's feet had barely touched the ground when the bus roared away, back down the hill.

A young man approached Tabitha to collect her luggage. As he ushered her past the gate, she turned around to see Tyler.

"See you on the other side!" she said.

Tyler waved back with a smile. A young woman walked through the gate to greet Tyler. "Welcome to Phool Chatti," she said.

"Thank you!"

"I take it that you are Tyler Morgan?"

"Yes," he said. "That would be me!"

"I hope you experienced calm and efficient travel."

"Oh, *so* calm! Are you Delta Diamond? It's unbelievable—and well worth the price tag."

"I am not, but I do thank you for the recommendation."

She guided Tyler through the gates, and Tyler saw the community of the ashram unfold before him. The buildings framed an open, grassy courtyard adorned with statues and small ponds. The buildings were almost a part of the mountains that surrounded them. They looked as if they had sprung from the ground. People in muted colors were scattered throughout the campus in various states of meditation.

"I am Aarti, and I am a spiritual counselor here at Phool Chatti. I am here to usher you into our ashram and elaborate upon your daily schedule. If you would please follow me."

She led him to the grassy field in the middle of the ashram. Tyler felt at ease under Aarti's observation.

"Your day begins each morning at five-thirty with the ritualistic bell ringing. You will arise from your assigned cot in a shared room with other novice students. You are encouraged to awake with a sense of purpose, using this time to focus and stretch at your bedside in preparation for the day ahead. At six, you will join your fellow students in the gathering hall for a guided meditation. This meditation is to be thought of as an expansion of your private meditation. From six-thirty to six-forty-five, you will practice mantra cleansing. You and your fellow students will be led to repeat sacred mantras to promote group cleansing. It is our belief that the individual cannot be cleansed if the group it belongs to has been contaminated. From six-forty-five to nine, you will be led in your private yoga practice. This is to focus on what you, the student, wish to achieve. We are here to listen and to guide. Your final destination is merely a byproduct of this practice. At nine, breakfast is served. Breakfast consists of chia, fresh fruit, and porridge.

"After breakfast, you are encouraged to go on a Walk of Contemplation. This is meant to be time to have with yourself and to reflect upon your growth, both short-term and long-term. Lunch is observed in complete solitude. Think of this time as an extension of your walk. You are putting energy back into your body after a morning of exertion and expansion.

"Group yoga practice follows lunch. This is your time to work together as a group of curious minds. You must share energy and strength with one another. With this opening of the group consciousness, free time follows. You are encouraged to collaborate with your fellow students. Painting, writing, and music are all encouraged activities.

"At four in the afternoon, you will engage in energy cleaning led by our masterful leader. You will lay flat as the healer will cleanse any negativity clogging your soul. Anything blocking you from growth. It is imperative that the spirit be most open during this daily ritual. You will attend Temple each day at six in reverence of the Hindu Gods. This follows the energy cleansing so that you are most pure in the Temple. Dinner is then served at seven.

"During the third week of your time at the ashram, you will begin collecting dry wood from the mountain during your Walk of Contemplation. This is in preparation for the Fire Ceremony, which will take place on your final night with us. It is our most sacred and cleansing practice. You and the other students will walk one by one to the fire, carrying a written declaration. A declaration of your biggest burden. What weighs you down. What holds you back. You will have prayed over this declaration in a divine consultation of what is preventing you from true expansion. You will throw your burden into the fire, allowing that energy to completely free you. And then ... your credit card was declined."

"What was that?"

Aarti held his credit card to her iPad. "Your credit card was declined."

"Swipe it again!"

"I did. Four times. Perhaps you should call your credit provider?"

. . .

Tyler stood outside the gates that had so recently welcomed him. With just enough of a signal, he called American Express. Both of his accounts, they told him, had been maxed out. He logged onto his Chase checking account—empty. He tabbed over to the savings account—not even a penny left. *Motherfucker!* He had completely drained his money by the time he left Italy. It was a miracle that Delta hadn't canceled his flights. It was all Amber's fault, he thought, his anger rising. When he told her to book him the trip of his lifetime, he thought it went without saying that he wanted the trip of his lifetime *within* his means!

There would be no fire ceremony. There would be no *love* in Bali. He was frantically trying to grasp onto any remaining shred of his planned trip. How could he have allowed this to happen? And yet, he couldn't accept that this was his fault. This was all Amber's doing, he thought. He knew. Why was he so stupid to place his life in the hands of some spoiled twenty-three-year-old? She had ruined him. Everything he worked for was gone. And now he would be forced to return to his liminal life. Would XYZ even accept him back? They hadn't parted on the most pleasant of terms. There was no possibility of working that way again. He felt he would simply die if he tried to.

What was he going to do? He couldn't afford a flight out of India, let alone all the way back to New York. Six years of nonstop work, and he had flushed it all down the drain. His heart began to race. He was in the middle of nowhere with absolutely no money to his name. Before he could think any further, he reached into his pocket and called Alexa, praying she would answer.

"Hello?"

"Oh my God! Hey. I really need some help. Can you look at some flights for me?"

• • •

His feet had blistered so quickly. The mountain felt even steeper on its descent. Tyler had to brace the balls of his feet into the oiled leather of his sandals. The friction rubbed painful blisters into the sides of the ball joints. The skin peeled back to reveal pink under-skin, raw with pain. He sweated through most of his linen, leaving sticky, scratchy patches of fabric glued to his body as uncomfortably as possible. The mid-afternoon sun beat down on him, and he didn't even have a visor to protect him.

If he had started his hike down at noon, it must've been somewhere around three. His bottle of water from the airplane was long gone, vaporized from his body. His suitcases anchored his arms to the ground. He barely had the energy to drag them down the rocky hill with him. Only one car had passed in the few hours, and it had blazed right past him despite his desperate attempt to flag down the driver for a ride back to the airport.

His feet shuffled through the gravel, and he did his best to ease the pressure from the blisters. He gasped at each sting, tears forming on his waterline. His throat ached with thirst. He threw down his luggage, and in an act of defeat, he sat down on the gravel, screaming into the palms of his hands.

"Those are some fascinating shoes you have!" a voice said.

Embarrassed by his tantrum, Tyler turned around to see a hiker, an actual hiker, decorated with all the certified accouterments of what it takes to successfully walk in nature. A hat, long sleeves, cargo pants, books, and a monstrous backpack. Tyler stood up.

"I'm a hiker by accident, not by choice," he said.

"Where are you headed?"

"I'm trying to get back to the airport in town. I have a flight to New York Wednesday night."

"Wednesday night?" the man said. "That's two days away. What's the hurry?"

"How long do you think it would take me to walk there? It doesn't seem like anybody is willing to give me a ride."

"Can't you call a taxi?"

"My phone is dead, and I have *literally* no money. My friend had to buy my ticket just so I can get back," Tyler said. He looked at the man. He couldn't have been much older than forty. His beard was peppered with gray hair. He looked like everyone's uncle, care-free and untethered. Tyler got the feeling that he was looking at his only hope of getting on that plane.

"So, how far am I?" asked Tyler.

"Jolly Grant airport?"

"Yep."

"I'd say you're about twenty miles away. You've got about

three hours of daylight left today, so I'd say get about three or four miles in tonight, and split the rest over tomorrow and Wednesday. If you do that, I think you'll get there right on time."

Tyler could see the man eyeing his current condition. His lack of actual footwear—and his now-ridiculous luggage—made him a pitiful sight.

"You're going to need some help," the man said. "I'm George, by the way."

"Oh, thank you, George. But if you could just point me in the right direction, I think I can handle it."

"Jolly Grant isn't too far out of my way. And you desperately need to borrow some gear."

"Really, that's far too generous of you. I can't accept it. But thank you!"

"I'm afraid you won't make it too far. Come on, let's lighten your load a bit."

"Well," said Tyler. "It wasn't my intention to also include *Wild* on this trip, but here we are..."

George joined Tyler at his suitcases. Unlatching each one open, George removed the clothes from the trunks, tossing the containers aside. They rolled up his clothes into tiny bundles that they stacked into a tarp that George had pulled from his own backpack. Ripping some strips of Duct tape, George secured the tarp to reveal a makeshift backpack. George taped some spare cables to the top and bottom, providing Tyler with some straps.

George took a step back to inspect his creation. Not bad. He rummaged through his backpack to reveal some cargo pants, a flannel button-down, and spare boots.

"Will some tens work?" asked George.

"Given the alternative? Yes!"

Tyler excused himself behind a tree to change into the outfit George had given him. He emerged looking like an actual hiker.

"That's more like it," said George.

They began walking down the hill, the sun casting forty-five-degree shadows on the ground before them. George passed him his water bottle and Tyler took a sip, restraining himself from the chug he so deeply longed for. The water felt cool in his mouth. Tyler let it sit for a moment on his tongue, swallowing ever so slowly.

"How long have you been doing this?" asked Tyler.

"This specific hike?"

"Yeah."

"About six months, I'd say."

"Six months?! Holy hell. It's been three hours, and I'm over it. Where all have you been?"

"Started in Nepal, and I've been working my way down the mountains."

"That's unbelievable."

"What can I say? You go where you're called. Have you ever hiked long distance before?" George asked.

"My senior trip after graduating high school, my friends and I did a two-day twelve-mile hike in Gatlinburg, Tennessee. It led to Dollywood. So, I'm not completely inexperienced."

"Dollywood?" asked George.

"Yeah, Dollywood. Dolly Parton's amusement park."

"That's not real."

"Actually, it is!"

"I cannot accept the fact that Dolly Parton has an amusement park named after herself."

"It's truly the most beautiful place on earth. Imagine Disney World, but instead of mouse ears and white gloves, it's blonde wigs and rhinestones!"

"Unbelievable."

"And here you are trying to make me feel like the ignorant one," said Tyler, laughing.

They kept walking down what felt like a perpetual decline. The angle was unrelenting and unforgiving. But the boots provided much-needed relief. Tyler swore to himself never to wear those cursed Birkenstocks again. An hour passed without a word between the two. Tyler almost forgot George was there.

He was getting lost in his thoughts as one foot went in front of the other, braced into the earth for support. The late afternoon sun cut through the trees on each side of the path, painting the ground in yellows and golds. It reminded Tyler of the woods behind his childhood home. He and his mother would go on little walks together when he was a child. She had always been so cautious of his adolescent asthma, swaddling him in scarves and jackets and mittens to protect him from any chill or gust of wind they might have encountered. She would absentmindedly hum as she held his hand. It was usually "You are my Sunshine" or "I'm a Little Teapot." Tyler would start singing along to her hum, causing her to take note of herself. She'd giggle and reach down to give him a hug.

"You're my duet partner," she would say before joining him in the song. They walked for what felt like hours. Tyler was now sure it couldn't have been more than twenty or thirty minutes —the woods behind the house simply weren't that big. They'd emerge at the path's end, looking at the back of their home. Back inside, she would make Tyler a snack of sliced apples and a dollop of peanut butter. She stood at the linoleum island and watched as Tyler sat at the barstool, dunking his apples in the peanut butter. She had a spare paper towel at the ready to wipe away any remnants that stuck to his cheeks.

"I'm a big kid, Mommy," he said. "You don't have to do that." How he wished he had her with him now to fix his mess.

"You said you're from New York?"

It was George. Tyler forgot for a moment that he was with him. He collected his thoughts. "Yeah. I've been there about ten years now."

"What do you do?"

"Do? Not sure. Did? I produced movies."

"No kidding? Anything I've seen?"

Tyler despised this question. He never had an appropriate answer. It would be so self- important to assume people had seen his movies, even if many had. If someone kept up even remotely with awards season, they would have heard of at least one of his projects, if not him. *Sleepwalkers* was nominated for Best Picture at the Oscars. This was the project that got him the most attention. And he was only twenty-five at the time. It was a terribly surreal experience, and now he felt so detached from it. Tyler couldn't gauge whether George had kept up with indie darlings, so he went with his safest answer.

"Probably not. What do you do?"

"Do? Not sure. Did? I was a therapist."

Oh great, thought Tyler. Just what he needed. He wanted to avoid any introspection while simply trying to survive. He needed to get to the airport. Anything else would be a distraction.

Left foot, right foot. Left foot, right foot. That was the mantra. "Where are you from?" asked Tyler.

"Calgary."

"Calgary, eh?" George chuckled.

"Have you been?"

"Calgary? I don't believe so. But we shot a TV show on Vancouver Island. So I spent some time with your people."

"Hey, I've visited some friends in New York before. Don't get me started on your people!"

"I do not claim those people as my own! I may have been educated in New York, but I was reared in southeast Missouri."

"You're a Midwesterner?"

"I wish. Maybe geographically, but where I'm from, it is very culturally the South. Actually, it's truly the mixture of the worst of both cultures. The absolute hatefulness and red-neck-iness of the South blended with the total repression and waspiness of the Midwest."

"Sounds great!"

"Oh, it's to die for," said Tyler. They stopped as the road Tyler's bus had driven up diverged from the trail they had been walking on. The path went straight, following the route of the Ganges.

"Care to take my way?" George asked.

And so they veered right and walked down the trail with no

other hikers in sight. *Left foot, right foot. Left foot, right foot.* The grass grew taller, reaching past the top of Tyler's boots. They stopped to spray themselves with some *Off!* The smell immediately brought back memories of Tyler's childhood. Warm summer nights at his grandparents' house, the whole family seated around a fire.

Tyler had fallen about twenty paces behind George. He did his best to pick up speed, but his breath grew short. This was the first bit of exercise Tyler had had in months. What a way to jump back in, he thought to himself. He despised exercise. He couldn't understand Leo's almost religious devotion to it. Leo never missed a morning at the gym. He dragged Tyler to a class about once a month. It rendered his muscles sore and useless for days. It would then take more convincing before Tyler would join him again to repeat the cycle.

Tyler's feet plodded into the damp earth. Clots of mud collected around the rim of his boots. The distance between George and him was growing. He needn't worry as long as George remained within his line of vision. Every quarter-mile or so, George would turn around and judge how much he had to slow his pace. Tyler was doing the best he could. He hadn't been so physically challenged in years. New York may be a walking city, but it was not a city of varied, treacherous landscapes, potholes and piles of trash notwithstanding.

As the sun began to set, their pace slowed considerably. They found a place along the river to set up camp for the night. George made sure they placed themselves far enough away from the bank in case of any potential rise in the water. George built a modest fire as Tyler assembled the tent. Once the fire was going strong, George boiled a pot of water atop it and made oatmeal. They sat on a log and shared a quarter bottle of Jack Daniels that George had been saving. They split a peanut butter power bar for dessert, clinking their caps of whiskey together in a toast. The glow of the fire warmed them, as did the jolt of the whiskey.

"What's waiting for you back in New York?" asked George.

"Absolutely nothing."

"So why go?"

Why would he go back to New York? He simply hadn't considered an alternative.

"Not sure," said Tyler. "My apartment is still leased out for another two months, and I'm pretty sure I've burned every single bridge I ever made there. I just don't know anything else."

"No family there?"

"No," Tyler said.

"Do you miss your job?"

He didn't. There was nothing about his former life that appealed to him. The thought alone of those days spent and wasted working at XYZ was enough to make him want to jump into the fire before him. His days began at seven as he gagged out the putrid burps of alcohol still concentrated in his blood from the previous nights. By that hour, Leo would have already returned from an invigorating poga class (a newfangled fusion of pilates and yoga that he never shut up about). While Tyler lay in a cycle-less slumber, Leo had showered, dressed, prepped, and left for work. After the third sounding of the siren industrial-set iPhone alarm, Tyler peeled himself from the percale sheets that had been purchased to supplement a PR-gifted Tempurpedic mattress, thanking Tyler for the product placement in *Sleepwalkers*. Tyler would meander each morning throughout the apartment in hopes that what needed to get accomplished would. From the shower to the closet to the kitchen, what little remained of a morning routine fell upon him through the fog of the still-running, too-hot shower.

By the time he would be out the door, he already screamed into his phone at Amber–fucking Amber... He wasn't naturally a screamer, or rather, he hadn't been when he first started working. It was a trait he acquired from bosses of yesteryear: a lingering inherited relic passed down by generations of toxic bosses. In fact, he hated yelling–it reminded him of his father–but in the performance of his career, it was required, and he complied even when no tension was needed. This meeting *must* happen before *this* meeting, or else *that* executive will know he spoke to *this* executive first and gave a shitty deal to *that* agent's client before *this* agent's client was even able to look at *this* project which was already too similar to *that* agent's client's project. And so on...

As his morning Uber arrived at the office destination cross-street of Greene and Broome, Tyler would extinguish three fires by igniting four more. Amber would have his first iced oat milk latte from his favorite Think Coffee on Bleecker perched on his desk next to any lingering pending signatures from the prior day's work with sticky notes attached like tumors citing exactly what he was legally binding his name to.

"Oh, shut the fuck up, Harold!" he screamed into the plastic of his office phone, "I am the *producer*, not the *writer*! It is not *my* job to be an endless fountain of creative inspiration. Unless you want me to take a writer's fee on this project! Oh, I'm sure the Writer's Guild would *LOVE* to collect some more fees from you! Is that what you want, Harold? HMMMM???"

As he finished the last sip of the latte, Amber swapped the emptied cup out for his second latte, having kept it chilled in the office refrigerator. Covering the receiver with his spare hand, he mouthed *YOU ARE A DOLL! I LOVE YOU!* before laying back into poor, useless Harold. Harold who miraculously continued to find work as a producer of critically-lauded films, which somehow managed to turn decent numbers at the box office. Harold who, somewhere, seemed to possess the same passionless need to be in the film industry. Harold who revealed that perhaps all the *energy*, all the *sacrifice* wasn't necessary to have a career. Perhaps it was just that: a career—never intended to sustain but rather to satiate. Whatever Harold's deal was, it only maddened Tyler more and more, causing the call to escalate into name calling before Tyler punctuated the disagreement by slamming the feeble phone back down on its receiver.

Amber would arrange an Uber to take Tyler to his obligatory lunch, where he courted and coerced some writer, director or agent into joining his latest project. They always took place at some trendy eatery below Fourteenth Street—perhaps Cafe Gitane or Cafe Select. Amber learned her lesson: absolutely *never* Jack's Wife Freda. Tyler found it impossible to say no to the ever-flowing cantaloupe mimosas. The sudden rush of sugar and alcohol caused an early-afternoon crash, resulting in an entire afternoon of pushed meetings and calls, thus causing an entire week's worth of scheduling to fall to catastrophe. All of that tragedy caused by a simple mimosa. During the meal, an inevitable and entirely-predictable crisis would arise where Tyler answered his cellphone to an incredibly apologetic Amber, who stated that he *must* hop on another call ever so briefly. He excused himself from the second half of the lunch without apology. By the time he returned, the food would be cleared and the bill was taken care of. Shouts of *THANK YOU SO MUCH* and *LET ME KNOW WHAT YOU THINK SOON, BABE* were exchanged on a windy downtown street as both parties slid into their respective rides and back to their respective offices.

At the office, Amber would craft an afternoon of back-to-back meetings: new projects to pitch, new talent to consider, new scripts to cover, and new hires to fire. Amber understood what the other assistants never quite figured out: to leave an unfilled thirty-minute slot in the calendar was to secure one's fate in the hellscape of one of Tyler's meltdowns. Nothing was more damaging to Tyler than silence, for those moments of nothingness contained spirals. The quiet allowed him to think and that was completely unacceptable. The jolt of business kept him on his toes—unable to ponder what might fall apart. So Amber kept his schedule packed; therefore, she kept his anxiety at bay—the hallmark of a truly great assistant.

Grinding through the afternoon, Tyler would require a third and final iced oat milk latte that Amber secured during her worked-through lunch break. By the time the sun set, he would poke at a half-eaten nicoise salad before dumping its remains in the garbage. Agitated and exhausted, he closed his office door behind him before waving goodnight at Amber, who still toiled away—or pretended to—over the calendar at her pitiful excuse of a desk. He would thumb over to Uber, plugging in whichever bar was the chosen destination of the night—perhaps ArtBar or Pieces. Anywhere with liquor and ambiance, really. He would blackout, somehow make it home, and do it all again.

They sat for a moment, staring at the fire crackling before them. Tyler took another swig of whiskey, grimacing. In the presence of George, his former life felt shameful—worse than shameful. Meaningless. All for naught.

"What about you? What's waiting for you in Calgary?"

"Not much," George said. "My wife and daughter died a year ago in a car wreck. So I came out here to be alone for a while. I already felt very alone in my life. And work became too much. As you can expect, being a therapist, it wasn't the most helpful occupation hearing other people's trauma day in and day out. And I was pretty lousy at it during that time. So I paused my practice and came out here. And that leads me right here to you."

"I'm so sorry."

"I appreciate that. You know, you'd think my experience as a therapist—specifically *grief* therapy—would give me some insight. But I don't know. It's an entirely different experience to be inside of it. I know the right answers. And yet, that doesn't necessarily mean I can learn from them. You know?"

The fire continued to crackle. Tyler watched an ant crawl up one of its outer logs. It was alone, with no nearby colony visible. It maneuvered just far enough to remain untouched by the heat, then it disappeared underneath the log.

"So what is it that you're running from?" asked George.

"What? Me?"

"Yeah, *you*. You don't just end up at an ashram in the middle of India only to learn you don't have a penny to your name."

"Oh, uh, nothing. Nothing. You know, just, just … life."

"Just life? If you say so." George stood up and stretched his arms toward the dark sky. "Well, I think we've had enough melancholic musings for one campfire. You sure you're okay sleeping outside on just the sleeping bag?"

"Thanks. I'll be fine."

• • •

The dream started differently than the others. He was sitting in a dark, wooded room. Tall walls of knotty pine reached far above his head. They continued upward into blackness without a restriction of a ceiling. He looked down to see that the floor was covered in orange shag carpeting. He heard footsteps and voices above him. He looked above again to see a ceiling now enclosing the walls. He realized he was sitting in the basement of his family's home on Lake Michigan. He had always been too afraid as a child to venture into the basement alone. The lighting was a lone lightbulb hanging by a chain. The must of mildew saturated the space.

He needed to get out of the basement. He ran up stairs and reached the landing. He could see the warmth of the living room just past the steps. He raced again, only to find himself arriving back at the base of the staircase. Without thinking, he ran again to the landing. He saw the dining table just past the next flight. He ran up a second time, only to find himself back at the basement floor, his bare feet chilled by the cold, dirty concrete. The footsteps above him grew louder. He listened again. It was Leo. He had no other reason to believe it was Leo than intuition. The voice grew clearer.

Help!

It was Leo's voice. He needed Tyler.

Tyler! Please. Help!

Tyler raced again up the two flights. He knew he'd reach the living room this time. Leo needed him. He saw him at the top of the stairs, his back turned. Tyler ran with all his might up the steps. Just as he reached out to hug Leo from behind, he found himself again in the basement. Leo laughed. His laugh grew until it was all Tyler could hear. It had been a cruel joke to torment Tyler, to keep sending Tyler to the basement again and again, and all for his sick amusement. The carpet's fabric gave way to sand, which slipped through his hands. He opened his eyes to see he was sitting on a beach. There in the distance was the house from Wellfleet. Tyler turned to the right to see the blue sea. He looked back to find the house was gone. He had been mistaken. He was on Lake Michigan. The Sleeping Bear Dunes sat on the horizon where the house had been. If he squinted, he could see tiny people racing down the dunes just like he had every summer growing up.

He looked toward the lake. About fifty yards out sat a rowboat. It looked like the rowboat his family kept at the house. He studied it more intensely. It *was* the rowboat.

Help.

It was a woman. A familiar-sounding woman.

Help.

It was his mother. She sat alone, lost in the boat, surrounded by violent waves. She reached out to him. She needed his help desperately. Tyler ran to the water and dove in.

Help.

He could hear her cry over the roar of the waves. The sky grew gray. He looked ahead and his mother was farther than ever. He couldn't stop. His mother needed him. She would die without him. So he continued to fight his way through the water. He looked up. The boat was much closer than before.

He called out.

Mom!

He got to the side of the boat, and she stood up, her back to him. He reached out his hand to her.

Mom!

Why wouldn't she turn around? He continued to wade.

She turned around to face him, finally. There she was. It had been so long. And yet, she looked the way she had in his childhood. She was so beautiful. Tyler cried out. Her left hand extended toward him. She was going to help him. It had been Tyler who was calling out for help. It was his voice, not his mother's. He extended his arms toward her. As he reached, a wave came crashing down on him, plunging him deeper into the water. He looked up and screamed as he watched his mother disappear from his view. He inhaled and his lungs filled with water. His body sank down to the bottom of the lake.

• • •

A rough tongue scraped against his cheek. Tyler swatted it away. It was Leo playing a little game to wake him up. Leo's tongue licked at him again.

"Leo, stop…"

The tongue swiped his left cheek and trailed up to his nose. "Leo, come on!"

He pushed again, but this time the tongue turned to teeth, and the teeth nibbled at his left ear. He rolled onto his back and opened his eyes. "What the…?"

Tyler jumped up from his sleeping bag, remembering where he was. It was a fox. He screamed again, scanning the woods for help. Startled by Tyler's screams, the fox cowered behind the remains of the previous night's fire.

George came racing from his tent, groggy. "What?! What is it?"

Tyler pointed at the shivering fox. George burst out laughing. Tyler stood, holding up the sleeping bag as protection.

"That fox!" Tyler screamed. "It tried to eat me!"

George raised an eyebrow. He bent down and held out his hand. The fox slowly crept over and sniffed at his hand. George gave its head a gentle rub. The little thing cooed. George smiled.

"He's not a fox," George said. "He's a red panda. They're quite common in these parts."

"A *red* panda? Doesn't that sort of defeat the purpose of a panda?"

The creature gave George's hand a small farewell lick, then hopped away into the brush.

They watched until it disappeared. "So ferocious," said George. "Pack up your tent."

. . .

Tyler was growing tired. They had to cover nine miles that day. They had been walking for about an hour and a half and were barely into their second mile. The terrain had grown increasingly difficult. Smooth grass gave way to unstable stones. What had been a lateral plain was now a dramatic downward slope. His blisters from the day before still stung, despite his new footwear. He had accepted some of George's spare gauze that morning and wrapped his feet tightly. With each step, he felt the blisters break open a little more, oozing out puss. The moisture seeped through the bandage. Tyler winced with each step. George lingered about ten feet ahead of him, showing no signs of wavering.

After an hour or so, George's pace slowed to a stop. He turned around. "Want to rest and snack?"

"Fuck, yes," Tyler said.

Tyler let his makeshift backpack fall onto the ground behind him. He sat down on the flat grass and unlaced his boots. As George retrieved some protein bars from his backpack, Tyler kicked off his boots and peeled back the socks from his feet. The blistered skin extended past the gauze and stuck to the sock as he pulled it off. Tyler unwrapped the gauze as quickly as he could to reveal the carnage. His blisters were red and raw, with white discharge collecting around the edges.

"Looks like you've got an infection," said George.

Tyler looked at him. "You think?"

George passed him a spare protein bar and turned to rummage through his supplies. Tyler unwrapped the snack and held it to his mouth. Before he bit down, he let it rest on his palate, absorbing the flavor of peanut butter and chocolate chips on his tongue. Saliva filled his mouth and submerged the snack. Once the bar softened, Tyler chewed and swallowed. It was too delicious. George produced a small white tube from his backpack and handed it to Tyler. It was Neosporin, the same goop he'd rub onto cuts as a child.

"It'll help you heal," George said.

Tyler squeezed the stuff onto his pointer finger and began dabbing it into the blister. They took turns drinking from a bottle of water, careful not to overindulge. Tyler had never felt so parched. He hadn't had more than four or five sips in the past twenty-four hours. Their supply was running low. Tyler shook the bottle to feel just how low.

"Is this gonna be a problem?" he asked.

"There's a water pump about two miles ahead. Think you can make it?"

"I guess I have no choice but to."

"That's not true. You could just die."

Tyler turned to George and broke into a laugh. George, too, laughed at the ridiculousness of what he had just said. Tyler laced up his boots and stumbled to his feet, and off they went.

Fortunately, the path grew less rocky. The altitude leveled out, and the trees bordering the trail had grown less dense, giving way to the July sky overhead. The sunlight grew more intense in little time. The air was thick with humidity, and Tyler was soon drenched in sweat. The dehydration was making him wobbly. He tried his best not to think about the discomfort he was experiencing, filling his mind with memories of Rome. *Oh John. I really think I might have fallen in love with you.* He imagined what it would have been like to move to Rome and be the proud stay-at-home husband of an esteemed paleontologist. What a pleasant life it could have been, Tyler thought. But no: he had fucked it all up in Cortona. And for some twenty-year-old who didn't even know what he wanted. He was so stupid to have entertained that little fantasy.

He pushed away thoughts of Italy and of John, the whole

situation too embarrassing to dwell on. Tyler had seriously fallen behind. George was at least a hundred feet ahead. Tyler tried to match his stride but failed to find the energy. He was so thirsty.

"Hey," he called out. His voice was weak. George didn't hear. He tried again. "Hey!" Still not loud enough for George.

He began to panic. His mind raced. What if George had forgotten about him? He kept his eyes on George's back, desperate not to be lost. He stumbled and found himself on his knees. He had tripped on a rock.

"George..." It was barely a whisper. Slowly, he focused his breath. He got up and his walk grew more steady. Oblivious to his pain, he accelerated his pace.

What're you running from?

That's what George had asked him the night before. A good question: What *was* he running from?

"Help..." George still didn't hear.

What're you running from?

It echoed in his mind. He felt himself beginning to sob from the exertion. He kept going.

The straps of his backpack cut into his sunburnt skin.

What're you running from?

He wanted to cry out. He needed to find the energy. He couldn't be left behind. He had to catch up to George. He tapped into a tiny reservoir of energy somewhere deep inside him. His life depended on it.

"George!" he cried out. George turned around to see Tyler, broken and running.

What're you running from?

"My mother is dead," he cried.

George ran to him.

"My mother is dead!"

Chapter Nine

It was that day on the beach in Wellfleet when Leo had brushed away the sand on Tyler's face to kiss him. Tyler could taste the dried saltwater on Leo's lips. Leo pulled away and Tyler stared into his eyes. They were hazel. He sat back and kept looking. He hadn't ever pinpointed the color. But hazel was what they were. They sipped sand-crusted cans of pinot grigio and absorbed the UV into their bodies.

Tyler was buzzed. A bit more than buzzed. The wine had finally caught up with him in the heat. His hand played with the trail of hair on Leo's abdomen. He caught Leo's eye and gave him a wink. He pulled him in for a kiss, sneaking his tongue into the corner of his mouth. His hand snaked under the elastic waistband of Leo's trunks. As he reached his shaft, Leo pulled Tyler's hand away, looking around to make sure nobody had caught them.

"What?" asked Tyler.

"Not here."

"Why not?"

"Because," said Leo, gesturing to nobody in particular on the deserted beach, "Because somebody could see."

"Oh, come on," said Tyler. He inched closer to Leo and rubbed his crotch. He felt Leo grow through his shorts. Tyler stood up and grabbed Leo's hand. He pulled him to his feet and dragged him to the ocean.

"What's going on?" Leo asked.

"You'll see," said Tyler as they met the ocean's shore.

Tyler lured him into the ocean, the water hitting just above their waists. Tyler dove down and pulled down Leo's trunks. As he reached for him, Leo pulled him back up.

"What's wrong?" asked Tyler.

"What the fuck are you doing?"

"Don't be so boring!"

Bolstered by the wine, Tyler dove down again and took Leo into his mouth. Leo must have been excited by Tyler's spontaneity because he came quickly. His taste mingled with the briney water. Tyler came back up for air and smiled at Leo, who stood there mouth agape. Tyler kissed him and giggled.

"Well, where has that been the rest of this week?" Leo asked.

"I thought you might like that."

Leo pulled Tyler in and held him. They kissed in the calm waters. Tyler had long denied himself intimacy, and it warmed him to be held. He'd tell himself that he wasn't built for sustainable relationships. He was a drifter, meant only to enjoy brief flings and anonymous hook-ups. It's what he had learned as a closeted teenager in rural Missouri. The possibility of an actual relationship hadn't occurred to him until he was in college.

They made their way back to the beach, hand in hand. The afternoon was slinking away as the sun neared the horizon. The entire trip, Leo had been annoyed by Tyler's inability to ignore his phone. Tyler claimed he couldn't miss anything for work. It would've been a disaster, he said. Tyler knew it upset Leo, who personalized it, as always, thinking that Tyler was prioritizing his career over their relationship. But Leo was guaranteed. Work was not. So it made sense to Tyler to prioritize his emails, constantly refreshing his Outlook and Slack. So it was that morning, one of their last at the cottage, when Tyler decided he would leave his phone behind. On their walk to the beach, he made a point of letting Leo know that he had chosen to go without his phone for the day. Leo hid his enthusiasm, saying that it was the *least* he could do to enjoy their vacation.

Tyler felt as if he were missing a limb. He kept checking his pockets for phantom vibrations, only to remember his phone wasn't on him. He tried to focus his attention on the day before him, refusing to give in to the anxiety of missing out on projects that were coming in by email.

The day had been so perfect. Leo hadn't been this happy with Tyler in so long. After all, it was so rare to have him free of distractions. They packed up their belongings, shaking the sand from their blankets and folding them back into their *New Yorker* tote. The setting sun cast a warm glow across the beach. The cottage sat at the end of a sandy path about a hundred yards in front of them. The reeds tickled their bare ankles as they made their way back.

"Are you excited for tonight?" Leo asked.

"What's tonight?"

"Jinkx Monsoon!"

Tyler had completely forgotten their plans. They were driving back to the Provincetown Art House to see Jinkx's one-woman drag cabaret. Tyler had looked forward to it all summer. He jumped up in excitement. Jinkx was his favorite queen to come out of *Drag Race*. Tyler even swallowed his pride and bought the meet-and-greet tickets, eager to thank her for all she had meant to him over the years. Tyler often came face to face with actors and artists for work, but this was different: he was ready to queen out for his Queen.

"Wow," said Tyler, "this really is a perfect day."

They reached the cottage and walked out to the back porch, which faced the ocean. "Want some coffee before we head out?" asked Leo.

Tyler had turned on the shower, giving it a few minutes to warm up. He undressed. "Sure, sounds great!"

His phone! He hadn't even considered checking it yet. How nice, he thought. He walked to the bedroom, where he had left it on his charger. He picked it up. *What?* He had two missed calls from his father. What could *he* have wanted? He scrolled down to see he had seven missed calls from his aunt Tina. She had texted him. His heart raced, trying to imagine what the fuck was going on. He clicked on the text from Tina.

Call me was all she had texted.

• • •

He wasn't even sure what an aneurysm was. It was some cold, sterile term he had vaguely remembered from *Grey's Anatomy*, but that was it. Little did he know it would be something so personal. Tina had spit it out between choked sobs. He barely understood her, but he knew what she was trying to convey: *So unexpected. She loved you. So, so sorry.*

He sat on the bed, still naked. No tears came. Just stillness. Leo walked in and asked what was wrong. Tyler didn't answer. He couldn't answer. His phone continued to buzz throughout the day. He assumed relatives and friends were calling. He never answered. He stared, unblinking, at the beach. He watched the waves crashing on the sand. They were constant and numbing, and he kept watching them.

Leo sat up with him all night, trying to comfort Tyler in his state of misery. At some point the next day, his aunt Tina called back. Leo answered.

"Hey, Tyler," he said. "You need to talk to her." Tyler reached out for the phone.

"Hello," he said, flatly.

"Hi, baby," she said. "Your father wanted me to call you. He—"

"Of course he did."

She went silent for a moment.

"Honey, the funeral is gonna be on Saturday, okay? You'll need to get down here. You don't have to worry about anything. I've arranged everything, okay?"

"Yeah. Okay."

"Okay, baby. Just let me know when you land, and I'll send Cody up to St. Louis to pick you up, okay?"

"Okay."

"I love you, baby."

"I love you, too, Tina."

He hung up the phone and handed it back to Leo. He felt like an actor rehearsing a play. It wasn't real to him. It didn't make sense: his mom had *just* been in New York the month before. He and Leo had put her up at the Public Hotel, where they had dinner together. He took her to Chillhouse for a massage and manicure. She wore clothes that Tyler had gifted her over the years but had felt too ashamed to wear in Dexter, Missouri. She wore the velvet SJP pumps, the Manolo mules, and the Acne denim jacket that had been custom-distressed by a friend who worked at the Blue & Cream on Bowery. It made Tyler so happy to see her happy.

Tyler had canceled his work lunches that week so that he could be with his mom instead. On her final day in the city, they went to Tea & Sympathy in the West Village. It was a quaint, English tea room with kitschy framed photos of the queen on the wall. The waitresses were eccentric, with shaved heads and thick, Northern accents. Tyler and his mom ordered jasmine tea that arrived in adorable, house-shaped teapots. They let it steep as they ate their scones with clotted cream. They laughed so much, thankful to have some time together. Ever since Tyler moved to New York, it was rare for the two of them to actually *be* with one another. Tyler was rarely home. Once, she had visited him on set during the shoot of *Sleepwalkers*. She sat in a designated set chair, headphones on, in awe of the magic that was happening around her. Tyler would catch her out of the corner of his eye and smile. All he ever wanted was to make her proud. And he had.

As they drank their tea, Tyler noticed that the middle-aged man sitting at the next table kept staring at them. It was obvious he wanted to say something.

"Excuse me," the man said. "I'm so sorry to interrupt."

He was clearly gay. *Jesus Christ*, thought Tyler. This man was probably some fan of one of his movies, and here he was interrupting precious time with his mother.

"I hope I'm not overstepping, but my mom and I used to come here when I was about your age. This was our favorite, special place. And it makes me so happy to see the two of you here enjoying yourselves. I just wanted to thank you. I'm glad to see the two of you enjoy it as well."

Tyler was touched. His mom was tearing up. She reached over to hold the man's hand. "Thank you, honey," she said. "That was so beautiful of you to share that with us."

· · ·

When Tyler finally got out of bed, he realized he was still naked. He made his way to his suitcase and pulled out some running shorts and a hoodie. He was hungry, yet nothing was appetizing. He was thirsty, but the idea of drinking water turned him off. He had temporarily forgotten that Leo was there, lurking in the corners like a house cat. He wanted to help Tyler, but there was nothing he could do.

It was Wednesday, their final day of the vacation. That meant three days had passed since he received the news. Leo packed and loaded everything into their rental car. When the time came to leave, Leo tapped him gently on the shoulder and gestured toward it. Leo opened the passenger door for him.

"Do you want me to book the flights?" asked Leo.

"Oh, fuck. I haven't even thought about that."

"You don't need to. But you should probably call your dad and work it out."

"As if this couldn't get any worse."

"I know, babe. But you have to."

Have to. That pissed Tyler off. There was so much he *had* to do. He *had* to go back to Dexter. He *had* to call his father. It nauseated him.

"Fine," he said.

He pulled out his phone and pulled up his father's contact. Leo gave his shoulder two small pats. Tyler's stomach was knotted—he felt as if he might retch.

"I love you," Leo said.

He squeezed Leo's hand and called his father.

Chapter Ten

God, give me strength. I need the strength to get back up and keep going. I see no other choice but to ask for your help. So please, please help me. Amen.

The water tasted sweet as it met his lips and dribbled down his chin. He felt a hand cupping the back of his head, propping it up. Slowly, he began to make out images: the blue of the sky, the dusty gray clouds, the tan trees. And there was George.

Tyler.

The sound seemed to come from far away.

Tyler. Wake up, buddy.

More water fell on his lips. This time, his mouth knew to swallow it. With each sip, his vision grew clearer. He could hear again.

He was laying where he had collapsed. George hadn't forgotten him. In fact, he had saved him. He was next to Tyler, crouched on his knees. "What happened?"

"Dehydration. You passed out."

They sat for a few more minutes, and with George's help, he was back on his feet. "Are you ready?" George asked.

"I'm ready for a hotel suite and a bath and room service. But I suppose this will have to do."

And on they walked, Tyler's legs trudging without thought. "So what happened to your mom?"

Tyler had forgotten. He had screamed. Just before he fell unconscious.

"Oh God. That's the first time I've said that."

"Said what?"

"It's the first time I've said … that my mother's dead."

George stopped walking and turned to face Tyler. He wiped the sweat from his brow, drying his hand on his shirt.

"The first time? I'm sorry, it must still be so fresh."

"She died two years ago."

"Two years? Oh Tyler. I'm so sorry, man."

Tyler started walking again and George followed behind.

"It was an aneurysm. Completely unexpected. I saw her the month before. She visited me in New York. And I didn't get the chance to say goodbye to her. I was supposed to take her to the airport, but a meeting came up, and I told her I wouldn't make it."

George placed his hand on Tyler's shoulder. "That's not your fault, you know."

"I don't know, though! I don't! I could've so easily canceled whatever the fuck it was that popped up. But I didn't. And she died a month later. She was my *everything.* She *loved* me. She was the only person who ever actually loved me! She accepted me for all I was. For all I am. And she's the one who had to fucking die! I just don't get it."

He planted his face into his hands to hide his tears. There was no stopping it. He heaved, uncontrollably. Slowly, he did his best to gather himself.

"I'm so sorry," Tyler said.

"There's no need to apologize."

"How'd you do it?" asked Tyler.

"Do what?"

"Live. Go on. What you're doing! How'd you do it after you lost your daughter *and* your wife? I don't get it."

"The same way you've done it."

"What? What does that mean?"

"I'm asking the same question about you. How have you done it? How have you kept going?"

Tyler stared at him. George clearly had something figured out. He was so poised, so calm. He never appeared to wallow.

Tyler would've assumed he was just some middle-aged man who had taken up hiking for sport after reading some GQ article about its positive effects on the libido. He didn't wear his pain for the world to see. How could George be asking himself the same of Tyler? Tyler was so pathetic. He was embarrassed.

"Tyler, there are no answers here. I have nothing to offer you except the option of standing here or going forward. That's all there is in this life. So what's it going to be?"

. . .

By the time they reached the water pump, they had grown dizzy. They drank and refilled the bottle over and over again before screwing the cap back on and heading back on their journey. The forest began to thin out, and small villages now lined their path. If nothing else, they didn't have to fear dehydration. George retrieved two power bars from his backpack and tossed one over to Tyler. They snacked as they walked, the sun less brutal thanks to some spare clouds shielding its heat.

"So how'd you settle on an ashram all the way up here?" asked George.

"My assistant—make that my ex-assistant—found it for me. I told her I needed a quiet, healing place to pray and do some yoga. So she sent me here."

"What'd you tell her the reason was?"

"Oh, because my ex dumped me. Not exactly out of the blue, I guess. I had sort of been daring him to end things for so long. I have a problem where I can't end a relationship. I never have been able to. I'll just keep going and going until it runs its course. I was a *really* shitty boyfriend to him. But I didn't want to be. I love him so much—he's a sweetheart. But he was there when I found out about my mom. And after that, I don't know, I just always—I associated that moment with him from then on. He saw my life stop that day. And he was so good, he wanted to talk about it, he wanted to help—but he couldn't. Well, I couldn't, at least. I never had that discussion with him. And that's when I started working as much as possible. And my drinking became a sport. I probably could've put Bette Davis to shame. Anyway. So the reason for this whole trip was because my boyfriend dumped me, and I felt so stuck in my life. And it's because I was—I mean, I am. And then I found this picture of me and my mom at the *Eat Pray Love* premiere, and of course I interpreted the movie as the sign—not my *mom*! And I'm sort of right now understanding that the sign I prayed for was my mom. I was supposed to deal with her. But I really ran in the opposite direction. And now I have no fucking clue where I'm supposed to be right now."

George finished his snack and looked at him.

"I think you're exactly where you're supposed to be."

Tyler stared at him in disbelief.

"You know, another friend I made on this trip said a very similar thing."

George took a sip from the water bottle and passed it to Tyler.

"Then I'd say that's a pretty good sign."

• • •

It was as if the fists that had choked him over the past two years had loosened their grip. His spine was a little straighter. His thoughts were a little clearer. George hadn't rushed him into any sort of forced confession. He let Tyler speak, putting the responsibility of sifting through his emotional negligence on Tyler and Tyler alone. He just listened.

They had been searching the past half mile for any break in the trees to set up camp for the night. They were losing daylight fast but didn't want to set up camp in the middle of the path. As Tyler's walk slowed, he heard something. He stopped to listen more closely. *What was that?* It was ... music. Music!

"George! Hear that?"

"Hear what?"

Tyler pointed to his right, in the direction of the sound. They both listened. It was *September*, by Earth, Wind & Fire. Tyler followed the music, and George followed Tyler. He pushed past the vines and brush, following the throbbing bass. And there, through trees, was a clearing. And there were people! They were dancing around a modest fire. There were five of them, and they looked impossibly happy.

"Hey!" shouted Tyler.

The woman who had been dancing nearest to them turned around. She wore a similar hiking uniform as they did—but had the luxury of a bluetooth speaker set up next to her. She smiled and bounced over to them.

"Greetings, fellow travelers!"

"Greetings," George answered back.

"What's going on?" asked Tyler, transfixed to be in the presence of other people.

"Come on, join in!"

She pulled Tyler over to the others as she danced. He grabbed at George to join them. Tyler smiled, not caring how he looked as he moved. It was freeing to be with strangers. They didn't know him, so he could just *be*. It felt like a blessing to stumble on this celebration. He spun and saw George dancing, too, smiling and bumping along to the rhythm. Tyler threw his head back and laughed. There was joy here. And it was impossible to ignore.

• • •

They offered George and Tyler some of their dinner. They had warmed up some cans of tomato soup in a saucepan over their fire. Tyler and George accepted their generous offer, both so happy to have something warm in their stomachs. Joan, the woman who pulled Tyler into the group, poured the soup into small ceramic mugs for them to sip as they sat around the fire. He sat next to Glen, Joan's husband. And across the fire were Steven, Toni, and Alice. Steven was about Tyler's age. His beard was thick, and he wore round, wire-rim glasses. He was adorable, and Tyler kept his eyes away, too shy to speak to him. Tyler assumed Toni and Alice were a couple—you could tell by the way they rested their heads on each other's shoulders. Tyler savored the first mouthful of soup, letting it linger to experience its full flavor. He had eaten only dried granola for the past day—George even longer. He couldn't imagine how much this offering meant to George. While the others looked away, Tyler dumped his portion into George's mug before he could protest. Tyler put his arm around George and hugged him.

"So what's the occasion?" George asked.

"Thank you for asking!" Joan said. "Today is my one-year anniversary of being cancer-free. I was told that coming through it would be impossible. Basically, I was a dead woman walking. But I didn't die. So, I've brought my husband and our three best friends out here to celebrate. When I was going through chemo, I read so many articles about the Himalayas. And I told myself I would make it out here when it was all over. So here I am on July Ninth, one year later."

"Oh my God," said Tyler. "Today is July Ninth?"

"Yessir. How come?"

"Today's my thirtieth birthday."

Tyler had completely forgotten. That benchmark he had dreaded for the greater part of a decade had nearly come and gone, and he hadn't even noticed. The day was like any other. Well, not *quite* like any other. But the experience of being alive in that moment felt more to him than so much of what he had gone through over the past two years. The day was nothing to fear. In fact, it was like any other. It just *was*.

The others searched each other's eyes, and as they met, they started singing, "Happy birthday to you! Happy birthday to you! Happy birthday dear..." They all paused, breaking out in laughter because they couldn't quite remember his name.

"Tylerrr!" sang George, allowing the others to catch on.

Tyler felt a rush of blood to his cheeks. He hid his smile in the palms of his hands. "Speech! Speech!" shouted Joan.

Tyler stood up, half-embarrassed. He shushed the group.

"Okay, okay. I want to thank you all for welcoming us to your party! My party? I am so honored to share in this cele-bration with you, Joan. Here's to you!"

He raised his emptied mug to the sky. The others joined in. Shouts of "To Joan!" filled the forest as they brought their mugs together and toasted with their tomato soup.

As the fire burned down, Joan and Glen returned to their tent. George had already finished pitching his own and was zipping himself up for the night. Alice and Toni soon retired to their own small tent. Tyler retrieved his sleeping bag from his backpack and searched for a place to unroll it in the grass. Steven sat around the fire and watched him.

"Hey, you know you don't have to sleep outside. It's cold out. I have some room." Tyler kept looking for a clean spot for himself.

"That's very kind of you," Tyler said. "And very *Brokeback Mountain* of you. But I think I'll be fine, thanks."

"You sure? There's no reason for you to stay out here. I promise I'm not trying to be a sleazeball or anything."

Tyler paused to face him.

"Okay, but just a warning, I usually don't smell like road-kill. This is a very new thing for me."

"If you say so," said Steven, smiling.

Tyler laughed and joined him in his tent. It was tight. The roof was vinyl and sloped. Most important: it was warm. Steven laid down on his pallet, and Tyler joined him. After days of discomfort, being in there was serene. It was as if nothing outside of the tent existed. It was just their private little fortress. Tyler wrapped his arm around Steven, and he accepted the offer. Steven snuggled into Tyler's arms and fit his head under Tyler's chin.

"Is this okay?" asked Tyler.

Steven burrowed himself into Tyler's chest. "Very okay."

And soon, they were both asleep.

. . .

There was a quiet sorrow to the morning. The goodbyes were brief—gentle pats on the shoulders and quick half-hugs. Their new friends were traveling north, up the very mountain that Tyler and George had just climbed down. Steven hugged Tyler goodbye, and Tyler held him tightly. They all thanked one another and parted, eager to continue on their journeys.

Tyler and George had only about six miles left until they were in town. They had made good time despite Tyler's inexperience as a hiker—and his fainting episode. By the end of the day, Tyler would be on a plane to New York, where he'd be forced to beg to get his job back. He would start over. New apartment, new friends, and new projects. And all thanks to Alexa. She had so generously purchased him his thirty-hour flight back to the city. He could camp out on her couch for a few days while he figured things out. He would have to take out a loan for security deposits, though he wasn't sure who would lend against him. His credit was destroyed thanks to his trip—a trip he didn't even get the chance to finish. He had just gotten started. And yet, he couldn't bring himself to care. He would figure out a way forward—he always did. This time would be no different. It would just be more difficult. But that was okay, he thought, because maybe there was something to all of this. All of what he had experienced. This sense of knowing kept him calm. And with that, he kept walking.

George spoke up. "So you're telling me that you're doing all of this because of a *book*?"

"Well, technically, a movie based on a book. But yeah."

George had a good laugh at his expense. He laughed until tears came.

"Well, the ladies in Italy were *far* more understanding!" said Tyler.

George did his best to collect himself.

"I'm sorry, I'm sorry! I've just never heard of such a thing. Why not just come up with your own thing to do? Doesn't that make more sense?"

"Because someone else already came up with it!"

"Well, that doesn't mean it's gonna do shit for you!"

"That is the issue I keep coming up against!"

"Do you even like the movie?" asked George.

"It's fine."

"I can't believe it."

"This is what I get for being vulnerable," said Tyler. "I open up to you, and you mock me! God bless your former clients, psychopath!"

George laughed, shaking his head in disbelief.

By the time they arrived at the airport that Tyler had been at just days earlier, he didn't want to say goodbye. George had comforted him greatly. He and George stood outside the terminal for a moment, just looking at each other, unsure of what to say.

"I do believe this is where we part," George said.

"I believe you're correct," said Tyler. "Thank you so much, George. This was all so unexpected. I wouldn't have made it here without you."

"Glad you couldn't afford that taxi?"

"The blisters on my feet aren't, but I sure am," Tyler said. They stood for another moment with each other as others passed to and fro. "How far left do you have?"

"Not sure," George said. "As long as I need."

They hugged. It reminded him of being dropped off at college. They hugged until their eyes filled with tears. They broke from one another.

"Thank you, again. I'll mail you back these shoes and clothes."

George laughed."Don't worry about it. You never know when you'll need them again!"

"I am thinking of never making another plan in my life," said Tyler.

George handed Tyler a piece of scrap paper with his number on it. "Give me a call sometime."

"For therapy?" asked Tyler.

"For a friend."

George gave Tyler's arm a pat and turned back to the road. As he walked away, the sun shined down beautifully. It reminded him of summer days out on Christopher Street Pier with his friends. When George reached the other side of the street, he turned around to give Tyler a final look. He waved. Tyler waved back and walked into the airport.

• • •

Thanks to a layover in Los Angeles, Tyler's phone was finally charged again. He waited for its Apple logo to melt away and reveal his home screen. He just knew there'd be a cascade of unread texts awaiting him. His phone was silent. He turned the airplane mode off and on, letting the phone reconnect to 5G. Still nothing. He went to his texts, and no new messages loaded. He refreshed his emails, but nothing came through. And so he took a deep breath and, against his better judgment, opened that garbage heap of an app formerly known as Twitter. He scrolled, uninterested in the onslaught of self-promotion and self-righteousness.

When he had landed for his first layover in Tokyo, he found a debit card in the back of his wallet that had gone unused for years. The account still had twelve dollars in it, so he bought himself a bottle of Poland Spring and a small bag of Lay's potato chips. Was it only a few weeks ago that he had been dining at posh Italian restaurants?

As he scrolled, one tweet caught his eye: "I wonder if Brian Williams gave Ashleigh Windham a ride in his helicopter when she was on her trip." It had over five thousand retweets and thirty-five thousand likes. Tyler squinted his eyes and read it again. The next tweet read: "Maybe the real sequel to Eat Pray Love was all the lies we told along the way." This tweet had gained even more traction than its predecessor. His timeline devolved into Ashleigh Windham jokes and death threats. He kept scrolling but failed to locate the source of the joke. He switched over to Google, searching for "Ashleigh Windham drama." He found a Daily Mail article and clicked on it. The headline read: *EAT PRAY LOVE 2 AUTHOR ASHLEIGH WINDHAM CONFESSES TO LYING ABOUT ENTIRE TRIP.*

In a teary-eyed video posted to her YouTube account, popular spiritual guru author Ashleigh Windham confessed to falsifying her overseas 'self-help journey' after evidence collected by amateur internet sleuths proved she had never left the United States. Photos surfaced of Windham partying at Hollywood's famous Chateau Marmont during the time she claimed she was abroad. In the video, Windham stated she was "embarrassed" by her lies and that she "lost control" of the story she was crafting in an online blog after failing to note that she never "actually went on the trip"—claiming that it was a "metaphor for her internal growth." Her publisher, HarperCollins, released a statement saying that it canceled her contract for her forthcoming memoir, Eat Pray Love 2: Eating and Praying and Loving My Way Through Life, *adding that it will be pursuing legal action against Windham to return her massive advance, rumored to be roughly $1.5 million.*

Tyler put down his phone. His heart raced, and he felt sweat accumulate at the edge of his hairline. He hadn't felt like this in so long. It was the feeling he experienced when he first read the script of *Sleepwalkers*. Something clicked. *This* was it! *This* was why he had gone on his journey. It would be his next project. He would option the life rights and turn it into the biggest, most exciting project his company had ever produced. He would pitch it to Jason, his former boss, who would be blown away by the brilliance of the premise. And he'd hire him back on the spot. Ashleigh Windham's story was his purpose. This was the story he was born to tell.

He dialed Jason's number as quickly as he could. His leg bounced up and down as the phone rang. It rang five times, his leg pounding hard on the carpeted terminal floor.

"Tyler?" he answered.

"Jason! Hey, buddy! Yes, it's me."

"Uh, what do you want?"

"Hey, I'm so sorry for the... erratic exit I kind of threw at you. But I took some time away and I've got it! I've got our next project. Have you heard of this Ashleigh Windham woman? She was some influencer who got canceled for—you know, I'm not sure what the reason was—but *anyway*, she got canceled, then she got canceled *again* for lying about re-creating *Eat Pray Love* and landing some massive book deal. You can't make this up. I've already got some casting ideas. I mean, Margot Robbie is the obvious—"

Jason cut him off.

"Tyler! Tyler, Tyler... Man, you've got to calm down. We've already optioned it."

"You've already optioned it?"

"Yeah, man. And it was Amber's idea. You know, your old assistant? It's her project. She has *really* come into her own since you left. She's, uh, she's taken your position at the company."

Tyler felt as if he might retch. The excitement that had filled his body was gone, replaced by a sense of doom.

"Oh," he said, finally.

"Yeah, man. I'm sorry about it. But I'm glad to hear you're alive, at least. Maybe we'll work together on something down the road when you get back on your feet."

"Yeah, Jason. Totally."

"Alright, I gotta run. Bye, man!"

Tyler sat there staring at his finished bag of chips. His fingers were greasy and coated in chip residue. He wiped his hands on his cargo pants, still covered with dirt from his hike. His head fell to his chest, caving in to the pull of gravity. He wasn't getting his job back. That was very clear. He tried not to obsess about the conversation he'd just had with Jason. It didn't bode well for what was to come. He had been so sure that this would be his great return to the film industry. Hadn't the signs been there? And now he had no idea of what was awaiting him in New York.

He waited for his boarding group to be called. Only a six-hour plane ride stood between him and his future. As he lined up and presented his boarding pass to the gate attendant, he felt a tremendous burden weigh down on him. He hadn't figured anything out. He wasn't returning with some grand lesson. All he had managed to do was *admit* that his mother was dead. He felt pathetic. He couldn't even grieve properly.

He had given up his career, drained his finances, and traveled thousands of miles—for *nothing*. He did what he could to push the thought out of his head. But he simply couldn't. He had been duped. The very impetus of his journey was a sham. A lie concocted to garner public sympathy. And he was the dumbass who fell for it!

He boarded the plane and walked to his seat, way back in Economy. He shoved what remained of his duct-taped, makeshift backpack into the overhead cabin. What few possessions he still had fit into the tiniest of compartments. He laughed at this thought and squeezed past the person in the aisle seat, then took his place in the middle. He fished a spare .5 milligrams of Xanax he kept tucked at the bottom of his wallet and popped it into his mouth, swallowing its dusty flavor down dry. He felt the pill carve its path down his trachea, scraping the walls of his throat, making Alanis Morissette proud. He closed his eyes and counted to one thousand, knowing that he would start to feel that cool ease soak through his bloodstream somewhere around eight hundred. He counted and counted, the rustling noises of his fellow travelers drifting farther away. Somewhere around seven-hundred-and-fifty, he drifted off to sleep.

• • •

Ding!

Ladies and gentlemen, the captain has turned on the fasten seatbelt sign. We ask that you return to your seats and fasten your seat belts. Thank you.

Ding!

Tyler's eyes floated open as the plane grumbled beneath him. He looked around to see eyes darting every which way. There was some sort of panic among his fellow travelers, but he didn't know why. The plane shook again, much harder than the turbulence that jolted him out of his induced slumber. His stomach sank. He shook it off and closed his eyes again, knowing it was turbulence and that it'd pass. The plane shot down again, this time more violently. Tyler looked down to see that he was white-knuckling his armrests. The woman to his left was in full-blown prayer mode. Her hands were clasped together, and she was mumbling desperate words to a higher power, tears cascading down her cheeks. Everyone in the cabin was now panicking, including Tyler. Was he missing something? Had some sort of announcement been made?

Ding!

Ladies and gentlemen, this is your captain speaking. We are currently experiencing an unexpected engine failure. Please remain calm and in your seats. Flight staff, please prepare the cabin for impact.

Screams erupted. Babies were crying. Adults, too. The cabin rattled violently as flight attendants ran unsteadily up the aisles.

"Impact!? Oh my God!" screamed a woman nearby.

Tyler pushed himself up, searching for help that would never come. His heart raced. He grabbed the woman next to him.

"Pray for me!" he screamed.

"Pray for *me!*" she screamed back.

They held hands and bowed their heads. The plane was falling at an unbelievable pace. Passengers' cries grew louder. There was an untamable unrest. It would all be over so soon, and there was *nothing* to do about it. Tyler had experienced this moment in nightmares, but nothing could ever have prepared him for this. It was all too fast. He felt his heart pounding in every corner of his body. This couldn't be happening. It made no sense. He had flown hundreds of times! There must have been something he could do. But what? Who could he call? He couldn't just sit there. He felt so powerless.

"Why is this happening?" the woman next to him called out.

The man to his right was motionless, crying softly. He looked resigned to his fate. He didn't even muster a sob. Tyler watched him for a moment, almost envious.

"Oh my God," the man whispered to himself. The man opened his eyes to see Tyler staring at him. Rather than turn away, Tyler continued to watch him. The man didn't look away either. They stared at each other, unsure of what to say. There was nothing to say. And then the man simply nodded his head to Tyler. Tyler nodded in return. He closed his eyes again and laid his head back. Tyler turned forward again as the plane roared and tumbled more violently than earlier. It fell again as Tyler let out a squeak of a scream. It sounded like a yip from a small animal. It was so foreign to Tyler that he wasn't even sure the sound came from him.

Ding!

"Ladies and gentlemen, we urge you to remain calm," said the flight attendant, her voice shaking as she spoke into the microphone. "We will be making an emergency landing at the nearest municipal airport—in Cape Girardeau, Missouri. First responders are awaiting our arrival."

"I'm going to die!" screamed the woman.

"I'm going to Missouri?!" screamed Tyler.

They screamed together as the plane hurdled toward the earth.

Chapter Eleven

Nobody spoke in the terminal. There was only the rustling of bags and shifting of shoes on the tiled flooring. Some people cried to themselves, still processing the rush of adrenaline and emotions. Airport workers distributed trauma blankets among the passengers, trying to comfort them. Tyler wrapped himself tightly in the scratchy wool as he held it over his shoulders. He couldn't help but feel just a *little* like Kate Winslet at the end of *Titanic*, when she stands on the rescue ship, shivering underneath her tartan throw. Before the plane's crash landing, fire crews had sprayed flame retardant on the runway. In retrospect, it felt almost unnecessary. There was nothing dramatic about the actual landing—it wasn't that much rougher than others he had experienced. It was anticlimactic in the best way possible.

Firefighters and first responders were there to escort them off the plane and into the terminal. There they sat, awaiting any updates on when and how they would resume their journey to New York. They filled Dixie cups with water from a drinking fountain in the corner. After about a half hour of silence, Tyler noticed one of the flight attendants standing on a bench. She clapped to get everyone's attention.

"Everyone! Hello!" She waited until all eyes were on her. "I know you're all waiting for some instructions. Now. A shuttle will pick us up here in the morning and drive us to Lambert Airport in St. Louis for a flight *tomorrow* night at ten."

The crowd moaned at the news, grumbling about having

to wait even longer.

"Now, now, settle down. I understand this is not ideal! Also, due to a local high school volleyball tournament, all hotels in the area are currently booked to capacity. Meaning we will all spend the night in this airport until our shuttle arrives. And remember, you will receive an email shortly asking you to fill out a brief survey detailing your experience on tonight's flight, and anything we can improve on. Thank you!"

"You've *gotta* be fucking kidding me!" Tyler said to nobody in particular. He *had* to get out of Cape Girardeau. He couldn't believe he was even there! He was all too familiar with the place, and had been quite content with the fact that he would never see it again. He whipped out his phone and dialed Alexa, not caring that it was almost two in the morning in New York.

"Hello?" she answered.

"Hey!"

"What now?" she asked.

Tyler was taken aback by her coldness.

"Um. Is that the way to talk to someone who literally just survived a *plane crash* and is stranded only thirty miles from his fucking *hometown?!*"

"What are you even talking about?"

"Alexa! One of the engines on the plane blew up! And we had to make an emergency landing in Cape Girardeau, Missouri—*of all places*!"

"Oh, you mean the plane I booked you?"

"What the fuck is that supposed to mean? Why are you throwing that in my face?" He paced across the terminal as they spoke.

"Tyler, you haven't even thanked me! And then you disappeared for three whole days without so much as a text or a call. That's what I mean."

"Okay, whoa! I can explain that. My phone died and I—"

"I don't want to hear your excuse, Tyler. I'm so sick of you reaching out only to get something. So what is it that you want?"

He stopped pacing.

"Alexa, I need your help. I need you to get me a car to St. Louis tonight so I can catch the first—"

"Oh, you *have* to be joking!"

"Please, Alexa," he begged. "Please, I promise, it's the last thing I'll ask before I get back. I just need to get out of here."

"No," she said. "What you need to do has been made *very* clear. You've literally fallen out of the sky and landed *in your hometown!* It doesn't get much clearer than that, Tyler."

"Alexa, please, come on. Just please figure out a way to get me back to New York ASAP! Please! I can't go home, you know that."

"No, I don't know that. What I do know is that you only care about me when you need something from me."

"Alexa, you know that's not true. I love—"

She hung up on him. He wanted to scream. Sure, he had been needy lately, but he expected her to understand. How difficult would it have been for her to arrange a car to get him to St. Louis? He could be on an early morning flight back. And then he remembered: what was waiting for him there? Nothing. And now with Alexa so clearly upset with him, he had even less than he thought. He didn't even have a place to leave his bags—his one measly bag—if he were to get back in the morning. He looked around the airport and saw his fellow distressed travelers trapped in this liminal space, hundreds if not thousands of miles away from their loved ones. They would all be so thankful to have someone a car ride away, someone who could come help them, he thought. And so, before he could think twice about what he was doing, he removed his phone from his pocket and dialed.

• • •

It was two in the morning, and he knew his father would have to wake up in about two hours. It almost made him feel bad for calling so late. Almost. He explained nothing, other than that his plane had landed unexpectedly in Cape, and that he needed a place to sleep for the night. He would get himself to St. Louis in the morning to catch the return flight. He just needed a bed for a few hours. His father said nothing more than "okay." He arrived in the same red Ford F-150 he had the last time Tyler was in town—about nine years ago. They sat in silence as they drove down Highway Sixty. The truck's heat was suffocating. His father always kept the heat turned on, no matter the time of year. It was a typical mid-July night in Missouri, porous with humidity. The passing landscape, a vast nothingness, was indistinguishable from so much of the rural South and beyond.

The truck turned right onto a gravel road just after the overpass in Dexter. This drive was well familiar to Tyler, even after all those years. About two miles down the road, his father made another right, and there sat his childhood house under the pale glow of the county light that stood near the house. It was humble, covered in vinyl siding, a brick porch out front. His father pulled onto the gravel under the carport and cut the engine, the headlights dimming to darkness. Tyler opened his door and hopped down. He followed his father's lead to the side door, which opened into the kitchen. It looked exactly the same. His mother's cookbooks still sat in the white cabinets underneath her decorative porcelain chickens. The peach-patterned blinds were over the sink. There, too, was the same small TV that kept Tyler company on so many afternoons after elementary school. How many episodes of *The Oprah Winfrey Show* had he seen? His father removed his Carhartt jacket and threw it on the dining table. He turned to face Tyler.

"There's some dinner in the fridge you can warm up, if you want something."

"I'm fine," said Tyler.

"Alright then."

His father put his hands in his jeans pockets and left the kitchen. Tyler heard his footsteps travel down the hallway to his parents' room. The door closed and he exhaled. He looked around for a moment, desperate to find something that had changed. Nothing.

He walked down the hallway, in the opposite direction from his parents' room. His childhood bedroom was at the end. He turned the brass knob to the right and pushed open the door. His left hand felt blindly along the wall and located the light switch, flicking it on. There it was. When he was twelve years old and casually mentioned the *slightest* interest in the St. Louis Cardinals, his parents were so excited that he expressed the mildest of enthusiasm for something in the world of sports—and outside of Mariah Carey—that they rushed to redo his entire room with a Cardinals theme. The walls were painted Cardinals Red, with the window blinds patterned with World Series wins. Bobbleheads of Albert Pujols and Yadier Molina lined his desk. A Mark McGwire-signed baseball was displayed in a Plexiglass box below his lamp. They had invested so much time and energy into redoing it all for him that Tyler didn't have the heart to tell them how much he disliked it. It felt as if he was in someone else's room, with their love of baseball, not his, splattered all over the room. He had liked the way his room looked before. The beige walls were quiet and unassuming. His bedspread had been creme and quilted, not cheap polyester with a screen-printing of Busch Stadium.

He walked inside the room to see it had been preserved in all its Cardinals glory. He tossed his makeshift backpack to the corner of the room. He sat on the edge of his bed and looked at his hands. They were filthy. He was filthy. Soil was caked under his fingernails. All sorts of bug bites and scratches dotted his forearms. He laughed for a moment, taking in the absurdity of his physical state—in this place.

He went to the bathroom and undressed. He peeled off

his clothes and unwrapped the gauze around his foot. The Neosporin had done its job. The redness had decreased, as had the tenderness. He turned on the hot water in the tub and looked in the mirror. He was a pitiful sight. His facial hair was patchy and wiry. Bruises and blisters painted his upper body. His shoulders had dark, rough marks where his backpack had chafed his skin. Three days of near-starvation had trimmed him down. His ribs poked through his sides, and his hip bones were prominent. He didn't quite recognize himself.

The water was warm enough and he stepped inside. It was bliss. He realized just then that he hadn't bathed since he was in Italy. He lost track of time. He had crossed so many time zones in such a short span that he had no bearings. The last time he had been home was in the spring of his freshmen year at NYU, when his grandfather died. It was a tense time in the household. Tyler was halfway out of the closet at that time. He no longer felt the need to be anything but himself around his parents, but he wasn't about to wear an Old Navy Pride flag shirt that so many of his fellows then wore. He was dating his first real boyfriend and hated having to hide his love from his parents. Friends noticed when Valentine's Day passed and Tyler didn't post anything. He explained that he didn't want to share anything online about his personal life. They bought it, which gave him a little breathing room. It shamed him to have such conservative parents. All his friends had open-minded, loving parents who celebrated their queerness. Tyler lied and described his parents as equally nonjudgmental. He didn't want people looking down on them. So he lied.

It was on the car ride back from his grandfather's funeral when he realized that if he didn't come out then, he never would. He kept trying to form the words on his lips, but failed. Before long, they had arrived at Lambert Airport, and Tyler still had said nothing. It was only after he collected his bags and hugged his mother that he said it: "I'm gay." That was all. His mother's face dropped. His father's was unchanged. It was that simple. Tyler nodded, took a breath, and walked to airport security.

His father never initiated another conversation with him after that point. His mother had come around, making amends. She grew to show her love for him more than ever before. She adored Leo. He was the only partner of Tyler's that she ever met. And now the only one she ever would. In those ten years, the only time Tyler had seen his father was at his college graduation, and even then it gnawed at Tyler just to see him that once. They didn't say much to each other. The three didn't even pose for a picture together. The only photo that existed from that day was of Tyler and his mom outside Yankee Stadium. He and his father corresponded only on birthdays with simple, meaningless texts devoid of any emotion. Tyler had tried to reach out, but his father never reciprocated. When he was at their hotel after graduation, he and his father were left alone in the room while his mom went downstairs to do some shopping in the lobby. They said little. Suddenly emboldened, Tyler finally asked, "Why do you hate me for being gay?"

The question hung in the air. His father, with his demeanor, sat there for a moment. And then, expressionless, he looked at Tyler and said, "My biggest fear in life was always that you were gay."

And that was that. There was nothing more to say. Tyler heard him quite clearly. He stood up from the sitting chair, said, "Understood," and walked out of the hotel room. In the elevator, he let himself cry, alone, his face in his palms. When the door opened to the lobby, Tyler was surprised to see his mom standing there as if she knew he needed her.

"Honey, what's wrong?" she asked.

"Dad! Dad is what's wrong?"

"What happened?"

She guided him out of the elevator and led him to the sitting area in the lobby. He sat down and she poured him a glass of cucumber water from the concierge desk. She handed him the cup and he drank it in one gulp.

"I don't want to ever speak to him again."

"Tyler, what happened?" she asked again.

"He said his biggest fear in life was that I'm gay. What's even the point of saying that? It's so cruel!"

She wrapped her arms around him.

"Oh, baby. Oh, baby... I'm so sorry he said that. You know, he's just funny about some things."

"That's an interesting way of saying bigot, but alright." She looked at him.

"Baby, he'll come around. He will."

"I don't know how you can stay married to him when this is how he feels about *your* child. You know, he doesn't even reach out on birthdays anymore. He truly hates me."

"Honey, your father doesn't hate you. He's a very ... he's not very emotional. Or he doesn't know what to do with the emotions he has, okay? I love him, I do. But you know I love you more than anything, right? You are my whole world, Tyler. And I love you. I love *everything* about you. But your father just needs some more time. I know he'll get there one day, Tyler. I do. We just gotta give him some time."

He hugged her so tight. She kissed the top of his head. "I love you, Mom."

"I love you, baby."

Tyler turned the water off in the tub. He pulled himself back onto his feet. He was so exhausted he thought he might not make it all the way back up. He walked to his bedroom quietly, trying not to make his presence in the house known. He pulled open a drawer to the dresser and searched for something that would fit. He found a T-shirt and some running shorts he used to wear to tennis practice. They probably hadn't been washed in a decade. He climbed into his bed, careful to pull back only half the bedding, leaving the other half perfectly made. It was a habit he had picked up when staying in so many hotels for work. It was easier in the mornings to make it nice. He didn't realize how tired he truly was until his eyes closed. Within seconds, he was asleep in his childhood bed.

. . .

He was disoriented when he awoke. It was like waking up in a dream. The red walls seemed threatening, and they burned even brighter in the morning sun. Tyler grabbed his phone and checked the time: eight forty-seven. Five hours of sleep. He would take it. Better than most nights in New York, he thought.

He slowly arose and creaked open his door. His father was long gone to the farm, but he was still nervous. He crept around the house just to make sure. He was relieved to find no traces of him. He needed to get out of the house. He felt trapped. He still had about nine hours to get to St. Louis. He decided he'd call his Aunt Tina. She would be more than happy to give him a ride. But he remembered she never woke up before ten. Not wanting to disturb her, he set an alarm on his phone with a note: "Call Tina." He peeked out the kitchen window and saw his mom's Camry still in its place under the carport. Opening the kitchen's built-in desk drawer, Tyler was pleased to find that the key holder still sat in the back right corner. He picked through the various keys, all belonging to farm vehicles and trucks until he found the one with the Toyota symbol.

The car's engine took a couple of tries to get going. It was clear the car hadn't been driven since his mom passed. Tyler wondered why his father even kept it, a painful reminder to see it there, unmoving. The car finally came back to life after his fifth try. He put the car in reverse and pulled out, desperate to get out of the neighborhood. He crossed the southbound lanes of Highway Sixty and made a left, heading north into town. The sky was gloomy, a mixture of grays. He hadn't checked the weather app recently but could feel a storm coming. He hoped the sky would be more clear up in St. Louis. He didn't want to face the possibility of another flight delay.

As he drove through Dexter's main strip, he decided to go where he always went when there was nothing else to do: Walmart. He pulled into the parking lot and parked in one of the vacant spots near the back: the last thing he wanted to do was socialize with someone from his past—and have to explain *why* he was back there.

He scanned the area. The lot was relatively empty, considering that it was the only Walmart in a twenty-five-mile radius. The only bigger one around was in Poplar Bluff, about half an hour away. Childhood trips to that Walmart in his childhood were reserved for special occasions, like going with his father to the gun section. Guns terrified him as a child. His father kept them all over the house: in the basement, in closets, in cabinets, in the garage, in bathrooms, in the pantry. Tyler only shot a gun once. His family was spending an afternoon up at his grandparents' property outside of Dexter. Tyler's father had bought a new twelve-gauge and was breaking it in with some target practice. Tyler was eight at the time.

"Tyler, come here," his father called.

Tyler looked around nervously at his mom and grandma before walking to the field where his father stood. His father handed him the gun. It was much heavier than he expected. His arms drooped as his father placed it into his hands.

"It's time you learned this," his father said. "Here, hold it like this." He set the gun's butt against Tyler's right shoulder. Then he placed Tyler's right index finger around the trigger and situated his left hand to caress the underside of the barrel.

"There you go. Now, look through your sight."

Tyler closed his right eye and used his left to peer through the sight. He felt his muscles quiver under the weight.

"Now, shoot."

Tyler took a breath and closed his eyes. He pulled the trigger. *Boom!*

The force of the shot threw him onto his back. He screamed out in pain, his shoulder aching.

"My shoulder, Mommy," he said.

"Oh, baby. We'll get you some Tylenol. That's gonna be sore." She turned to his father.

"Don't you see he's too young to handle a gun like that?"

"Hell, hon. I was shooting when I was younger than him!"

"Well, clearly, this is not an interest of his."

"Then it's about time it is!"

• • •

Tyler found himself in the chips aisle, wandering absentmindedly. He was only there to kill time.

"Tyler Morgan?" said a voice.

His stomach dropped. He slowly turned to see which ghost of his past was haunting him in the Walmart chip aisle.

"Yes?" he asked. "Oh my God!"

It was Katie Langley! They had been best friends throughout middle school and high school. She was his only saving grace during those years. They did everything together. It was during seventh-grade government class that their friendship was solidified. It was 2004, and they were the only two people in the class's mock election to speak out against George W. Bush. The pariahs of the class, they quickly fell into a beautiful friendship. And then Tyler left Missouri. And he lost his friendship with Katie. They texted on and off, but what they shared in common faded over time.

"Katie! How are you?"

He hugged her. Her figure had filled out since he last saw her. Her hair was cut short. She looked so grown up. As he no doubt did to her.

"What are you doing here?" she asked.

"Oh, Jesus. That's too much for the Walmart chip aisle."

"Are you visiting your dad?"

"Um. That's not really the word I'd use for it, no."

She laughed. She got it. She understood his relationship with his father.

"I'm almost finished here. I don't know what you've got planned, but I'm free until three when I pick up the kids from daycare."

"Kids?! Katie! Oh my God!"

Tyler had never considered reproduction, let alone parenthood. It stunned him to see someone his age so settled in actual life. Heterosexual life. It wasn't something he gave much thought to.

"Yes, kids! Two of them. Can you believe it?"

"No, I really can't. That's wild!"

She shook her head and smiled.

"Well, I'm down for whatever," Tyler said. "I'd love to catch up."

"Great! Let me check out. Then wanna follow my car back to my house? I guess it's way too early for lunch!"

Tyler walked back to the Camry and hopped in. He scanned the local radio stations for something other than male country or contemporary Christian, but came up dry. He watched Katie push her cart through the automatic doors and unload her seven plastic bags into the back of her SUV. Her car was nice, one of those luxury SUVs, incognito minivans for moms with means. It was a Mercedes. He didn't even know there was a Mercedes dealer anywhere near Dexter. She probably had to drive all the way to St. Louis just to get the oil changed, he thought. She pulled out of the parking lot and Tyler tailed behind. They passed through town and headed out north. Tyler realized he didn't even know where she lived. He didn't even know who her husband was, if she had one.

They made a right onto what used to be vacant farmland and was now a developed neighborhood. Katie stopped at a barrier and tapped in a number. The solar-powered gates opened up and Tyler scooted behind her. The homes were ones you'd see HGTV promote: farm-style, black-roofed, multi-level houses with faux-craftsman columns on the front porches. Each door featured a plank of wood with a hand-painted WELCOME or HOME sign, some adorned with twiggy wreaths. Tyler recognized the style immediately. It was so *Magnolia*, so *Pinterest*. But he stopped himself—he didn't want to judge. These people had families, they had homes. He couldn't say the same. They belonged to somewhere and to someone. Maybe they didn't rub elbows at Sundance with Rihanna's cousin. Maybe they didn't take ecstasy in a Laurel Canyon midcentury modern before descending into West Hollywood for cocktails and group sex. Maybe they didn't produce movies. But he did, and he was unhappy.

He followed Katie into the garage. Loose soccer balls and t-ball bats littered the floor, evidence of young children. Katie opened the door to the house, holding it for Tyler. "Here we are," she said.

The house was exactly as he had pictured. The walls were accentuated with shiplap and decals instructing those who lived there to "Live, Laugh, & Love." Above the Keurig in the kitchen was a sign that read, in playful letters, "Coffee." Katie invited him into the living room, where he sat in a cushiony, oversized love seat.

"So what have you been up to?" she asked. "Still making movies?"

"Not exactly. About a month ago, I took a step back to just take some time for myself."

"That's good. I don't know how you kept working so much after your mom..."

"Yeah, I know. I don't either... So, what have you been up to? Also, who the hell did you marry?"

She laughed.

"You really don't ever look at Facebook, do you?"

"I'm sorry, I'm not trying to get recruited into some alt-right militia!"

"I married Hunt Worley four years ago," she said.

"Woah! Hunt? Tell me everything!"

And so she did. She explained how she and Hunt had run into each other one weekend at a Blues game in St. Louis. Katie was there with some sorority sisters from Mizzou. Hunt was shadowing the team's physical therapist. He had grown into manhood. And she told him how quickly they fell in love. And how she married him and moved back to Dexter, finding work as a social worker at the local women's shelter. And how one year into their marriage, she gave birth to their daughter, Paige. And then, two months after giving birth, she found out she was pregnant with their son, Christian. And she told him how tired she was, and of how much she judged herself. For not being the perfect mother. For not knowing how to maintain herself while raising children. While keeping her marriage sustained. But she was happy, she said. She really was. And before Tyler knew it, they had picked up right where they left off all those years ago. He told her of his successes and failures, both personal and professional. And they reminisced. That time they went to Dollywood after graduating high school. The Katy Perry concert they attended right before Tyler moved to New York. The karaoke nights they snuck into under age at Buffalo Wild Wings. And as they sat there talking, Tyler felt himself yearning. Yearning for what this friendship could've been if he would've tried harder. If he would've tried at all. But Missouri would always be the closet for him. New York would be freedom. He didn't know how to reconcile the two versions of himself. So he didn't. Sitting there, looking at Katie and all she had accomplished, he wished he had. It would have been worth it. The morning slipped by into noon as they talked. Katie threw together a salad and offered Tyler some. It wasn't until about two in the afternoon that Tyler remembered his flight.

"Oh shit!" he said.

He pulled out his phone and went to his alarm. He had set it for ten a.m. tomorrow, not today. *Shit!* Even if he left right then, it would put him in St. Louis without enough time to make it through security and boarding. And he hadn't even called Tina yet to ask for a ride.

"What is it?" asked Katie.

"I think I just accidentally stranded myself in Missouri for the night. I'm going to miss my flight back to New York."

"Do you need a place to stay? You're more than welcome to stay here for the night!"

"Actually?" he asked.

"Yes, of course!"

"That's so nice of you. Thank you."

He couldn't go back to his father's house. He had nothing to say to him. And there was no way he could admit any sort of defeat to him. His father would pity him, lecturing him on the importance of maintaining a schedule. He refused to give his father that gratification. He would call the airline in the morning and explain his situation. They would give him whatever he requested. They had almost killed him twelve hours earlier! The thought of staying the night at Katie's wasn't so terrible. He loved getting to catch up with her. There was great comfort in her presence. She actually knew who he was. There was no pretense. There was no performance. And it'd be nice to see Hunt as well. They were friends in elementary school, but sports took Hunt in one direction, and the lack of sports took Tyler in another. Hunt was one of his friends who had terrorized him with paintball guns.

Tyler rode with Katie to pick up Christian and Paige at daycare. They were at that age when they accepted anything. When they climbed into the back of the car, they didn't bat an eye at Tyler's presence. Katie introduced them to Mommy's old friend. Paige waved at him while Christian gave him a high-five. They played on their iPads as they drove through town. By the time they arrived back at the house, both kids rushed out to go play on their trampoline.

When Hunt arrived home from work, Katie explained everything to him. Tyler and Hunt hugged and laughed over the situation. Tyler fought the urge to deepen his voice and straighten his wrists around Hunt. It was a whir of forgotten memories. And now Tyler wanted to make up for lost time. He was determined to become more engaged. He would learn Christian and Paige's birthdays, sending them extravagant gifts each year. He wanted to be known as "Uncle Tyler." He would invite Katie and Hunt to come stay with him in New York, or wherever he ended up. They would go out to a ridiculously overpriced dinner in some downtown restaurant where it would be *impossible* to score a reservation, yet Tyler would ask some old fling or former colleague to pull a string, and he'd come through. He wanted to be the person he was destined to be before he ran away from himself. He was suddenly flooded with regret. Here were two people who had cared so deeply for him, and for whom he had once cared deeply. And he traded that for what?

Katie poured him a generous glassful of Bota Box Red Blend wine. He nursed it as he helped Katie prepare baked ziti as the kids played upstairs in their toy room. Hunt drank a Michelob Ultra and washed the dishes as they cooked. They laughed and reminisced. Tyler felt more content than he had in recent memory. Something felt right as he stood at the marble island listening to the kids roughhouse. Something seemed to align within himself. Hunt flirted with Katie as she popped the dish into the oven. The family gathered in the dining room, where Tyler sat across from Katie and next to the kids. Before they ate, Hunt said, "Shall we pray?"

Chapter Twelve

It was noon the next day and he still hadn't called the airline to change his flight. He kept flirting with the idea, his thumb hovering above the dialed-in number, refraining from touching the call button. He left Katie's after breakfast, not wanting to overstay his welcome. He needed to get his bag from his father's house. As he jiggled the front door, he realized he didn't have a key. He sat in his car for about an hour, hoping maybe his father would come home early or grab his lunch—or something. As lunchtime came and went, he knew he'd have to drive down to the farm and get the keys himself. He needed to come up with an explanation for why he was still in town.

He passed his elementary school on the drive. There on the corner was the music room, its window still cracked. His elementary music teacher, Mr. Winters, had been a hippie, teaching the kids to sing protest songs by Sixties folk singers. He'd play albums and let the kids sing along, offering them tambourines and drums to keep the beat. Tyler's favorite had been Odetta at Carnegie Hall. There was one song that always struck him:

Sometimes I feel like a motherless child,
Sometimes I feel like a motherless child,
Sometimes I feel like a motherless child,
A long way from home...
A long way from home...

Even back then, it meant something to him. He didn't possess the vocabulary to express why—he didn't to this day. But it was a song he had long forgotten. And now, driving out to meet his father, he found himself singing it. Something about the melody soothed him. He was driving his mom's car, so close to home. But it wasn't home. It really never had been. He thought of the town and felt nothing. But where *was* home? Where was that plot of earth he called his own? He crossed the backroad onto his father's farmland. He looked around and saw nothing for miles. Just row after row of soybeans. There was a tractor way back in a far field. It was probably a farmhand. His father usually plowed in the mornings and then dealt with the monotonous business side in the afternoon. Or at least that had once been his schedule. Tyler kept driving toward the main barn where his father's office was located. It sat off a dirt road about two miles into the farm.

It hurt too much to try to take in the state of his mom's car. It felt like a gallery display of her undisturbed life: her lipstick in the cupholder, her sunglasses in the passenger seat, her purse by the passenger door. He didn't let himself absorb any of it. He pretended it wasn't there.

He parked outside the barn and walked inside through the massive garage door that had been left open. It was a metal structure with a high-beamed ceiling where various birds had made their nests over the years. He walked to his father's office, an awkwardly built shed-like structure that sat in the corner. He knocked on the door frame before entering.

"Hey," said Tyler.

His father wore reading glasses while looking over various forms and bills laid out before him on the desk. He was surprised to see Tyler standing there.

"I thought you left."

"There's been a mix-up with my flight. I need to stay here a few extra days, if that's alright."

His father's attention returned to the paperwork. He shuffled through the papers. "Yeah, that's fine," he said.

"Okay, great. Thanks." Tyler stood there while his father paid him no attention. "Can I have the keys to the house, please?"

His father looked up from his desk and gestured toward the table in the corner of the room.

"Sure, over there," he said.

"Thanks," said Tyler, snatching the keys from the table, "See you later."

His father said nothing as Tyler exited. He walked through the barn, his feet shuffling across the concrete floor. He still wore George's boots, the only shoes he possessed. He yearned for the Birkenstocks he had deserted on that Himalayan hillside. They were far more comfortable and didn't drag as dramatically as the boots. But the boots had been a beautiful gift. A much-needed gift. He smiled at the thought of George's kindness. Tyler climbed back into his mother's car, turned the key, and drove back to his childhood home.

• • •

Tyler heard his father come in through the side door. He holed up in his bedroom all evening, dreading his father's arrival. He heard him lumbering throughout the kitchen before plodding down the hallway. He heard the door shut, and he exhaled again. He knew that once his father was in his room for the night, he was in the clear. Tyler quietly opened the door and crept to the kitchen. He was starving—he hadn't eaten since that morning at Katie's, where she fed him oatmeal and black coffee.

He rummaged through the refrigerator. All he saw was a jar of pickles, some condiments, Kraft singles, and a half-pitcher of iced tea. He closed the fridge and opened the pantry. He combed through the soups and ramen noodles for something—anything—that looked appealing.

"Do I even want to know where you've been?"

Tyler jumped. He turned around to see his father standing there in his work clothes. He must've left his room as Tyler was scanning for food. His father wore a face of apathy. Age had worn fine lines deep into his face. His skin was dark and leathery from years of working in the sun.

"What the hell is that supposed to mean?" said Tyler, his arms crossed.

"I just meant by all the—. Oh, never mind."

"Oh, sure. 'Never mind' your obvious homophobia. I could never do anything without—"

"Homophobia? How in the world? Is that what you—"

"Well, that's what it always is with you, isn't it? Hmm? Because you can't push your fucking brain to look past—"

"I am not going to stand here and be cussed at by the boy who wouldn't even show up to his own mother's funeral!"

It was as if he had punched Tyler in the stomach. He tried to respond but couldn't. How dare his father.

"That's how you remember it?" asked Tyler, his voice wavering.

"It needed to be said."

"Oh, it *needed* to be said? Sure, a fucking lie is what needed to be said!"

"A lie? And *please* stop that cussing. I can't—"

"I can't believe that's the story you've been telling yourself," said Tyler. He paced back and forth in front of the refrigerator. "That's what you think! That I just couldn't be bothered to show up to my mom's funeral!"

"*Please* then, Tyler. If you're so smart and so educated and so understanding and open-minded. *Please* tell me what actually happened!"

"You told me I couldn't bring my goddamn boyfriend!"

There it was. Out there, sitting between the two of them for both to see in all its ugliness. That rotted, tarry ball of pain, of resentment, that he had been holding in. It was out there now, and there was no putting it back where it came from. His father stared at him, his eyes sharpening. Tyler felt something gurgle up from deep within himself. His throat constricted and he could feel blood rush to his face. He wanted so terribly to cry—there was nothing more he wanted to do. But he refused to give his father that reaction. He would not allow him to see the pain he had caused him. What Tyler had said was enough: the truth. His father would have to deal with it, but he wouldn't give him tears. He wasn't worth it.

"She wouldn't have liked that," his father said quietly.

"Yes, she would have. She *loved* him. You're the one who refused to meet him. You're the one who missed out. And I will always have that experience with her. You're the one who missed out on what it actually was to have a family."

"I didn't see the purpose in meeting him," his father said.

"Well, clearly she did. So don't throw that shit on me as if you're a victim here."

Tyler left his father standing there in the kitchen and walked to his bedroom. He closed the door behind him, pressing himself against it. He listened for anything. After about five minutes, he heard his father walk to the living room, turn on the television, and watch the evening news. As if nothing happened.

• • •

His overhead light clicked on as his eyes drifted open. It was still too dark outside to be awake. He looked to the door to see his father standing there, hand on the light switch.

"What's going on?" asked Tyler, half-asleep.

He rubbed the corners of his eyes and rolled over.

"I'm down a farmhand and need help," his father said. "You want to sleep here, you're working."

"How come you're down a farmhand?" he asked, buying some time.

"Joe's out on paternity leave."

"I'm surprised you even recognize that term, let alone honor the concept."

"My truck is pulling out now. You've got half an hour to get there." His father shut the door.

Tyler looked at his phone to see the time: four-fifteen. He rolled face-down into the pillow and let out the largest groan he could muster.

• • •

The sun cut across the land as he steered the combine through the north pasture. It was muscle memory, something he had been taught as a young child. He was thankful this combine had been upgraded to feature an entire indoor cabin with air conditioning to relieve him of the unbearably humid July day that surrounded him. He was probably fifteen or sixteen the last time he drove a combine through these fields. It wasn't something he imagined ever doing again. In just a few short months, the temperature would drop, and this very field would be flooded waist-high to provide a place for hunters to congregate for duck season. A small hut constructed with plywood and tarps would be erected in the middle of the artificial swamp with an open slat left in the roof to slide the barrel of a shotgun through, aimed at the ducks flying above.

Only once did Tyler accompany his father to the duck blind. It wasn't long after the time when his father forced him to shoot the gun. They awoke early, earlier than a day at the farm, around three-forty-five, when it was more night than morning. Tyler wore waterproof waders over his nylon track pants, the coveralls sliding over his shoulders. He slipped into his puffy, camouflaged jacket, joining the Velcro patches on the front to keep out the cold. His father had already warmed the truck by the time Tyler climbed inside. They drove out quietly to the field, his father cutting the lights about a quarter-mile out to prevent scaring away any flocks. Tyler hopped out of the truck and kept close to his father's side. His father bent down and picked him up, placing him over his shoulder. Tyler rested there as his father eased into the drowned field, his gun slung over his other shoulder. His father waded out into the water. It reached up to his navel. From Tyler's view over his father's shoulder, he watched ripples spill out from his father's movement, echoing throughout the dark water. They reached the duck blind, and his father opened the makeshift door. Tyler climbed inside. They sat there waiting for any sound of a migrating flock as the moonlight faded dimmer and dimmer with the foreboding day.

Just before sunrise, there were distant quacks. They grew louder as Tyler searched the sky for their appearance. He adored ducks at that age. He and his mother would go to his grandfather's pond each weekend and feed them slices of bread as they swam to the edge to greet them. Tyler would giggle as their tiny bills would snap at the bread in his hand, tickling his palms. As the flock flew overhead, his father cocked his shotgun.

Bam!

Tyler hadn't even prepared his ears. The shot rang through his head, then ricocheted throughout his body, sending a shake down his spine. A single duck fell from the sky and smacked the waterline about fifteen feet ahead of the blind. His father left the shack and waded through the water to collect his bounty. As he brought it back into the blind, Tyler stared at it. It was still alive. Its breath was heavy and laborious. He watched its chest expand with great effort and stall there before releasing the air to repeat the strenuous process. His father placed it on the plywood floor as blood trickled out from behind its wing. The blood met and mingled with the muck water on the blind's floor. The smell of the iron and sediment nauseated Tyler. He wanted to help the poor thing. It had survived for a reason, he thought. As he reached out to comfort it, his father stopped him gently and shook his head no. Tyler watched as his father placed his boot on the duck's head and applied pressure. As he pressed, one long *quaaack* escaped the duck's bill before his father crunched into its neck. The sound stopped as Tyler watched his father remove his boot from the duck. He went home that morning and cried into his pillow.

It was two p.m. as Tyler pulled the combine back into the barn. He hopped down from the tractor's cab and wiped the dirt from his hands onto his Carhartt pants.

"Hey," his father said from the opened door to his office.

"Hey," said Tyler, walking over to the office.

"Wanna grab some lunch? I'm about to head out of here."
Tyler wasn't sure what to make of the invitation.

"Um, sure. Where are you going?"

"I was thinkin' Myrtle's. That work for you?"

"Yeah," said Tyler. "That works for me."

• • •

Myrtle's looked just as it had all those years ago. It was the town's signature greasy spoon, known for its barbecue, and photos of pigs and pig statues filled the room. Fox News played continuously on the television in the corner. Pete, their waitress, had worked there for decades. Her platinum-dyed hair was permanently crunchy from years of hairspray. Her arms were rail-thin and smattered with liver spots from years of smoking. She hustled up and down the aisles, delivering platters and plates, only pausing to refill cups of black coffee. She approached their corner booth with a pot in one hand and a tray in the other.

"Hey, boys!" she greeted them. "I have Big Debbie's special: eggs over easy for you, Ed."

She placed the heaping plate of grease in front of his father.

"And I have biscuits and gravy with a side of hashbrown delight for you, baby," said Pete, presenting Tyler with his order. "Can I get y'all anything else?"

"I think we're good, thanks," said Tyler.

"Alright, y'all. Give me a holler if you need anything!"

Tyler separated his biscuits into halves and poured the bowl of white sausage gravy over the biscuits.

"Same order," said Ed.

"What's that?"

"It's the same order you had when you were a little kid. I'm surprised you're not one of them *vegans* by now."

"That was three years ago. Not enough iron. I passed out in SoulCycle."

"Is that a church?" asked his father.

"Sorta."

Tyler took the first bite of his biscuits. They were divine. It was the kind of gravy that can only be created with fried animal fat. He had deprived himself of it for so long. He always felt the risk outweighed the reward. And besides, biscuits and gravy did not grace most New York City menus. He cut a corner off his hash brown delight and placed it on top of a bite of biscuit. It was his favorite way to eat them as a child.

"How's the city been?" Ed asked.

"Oh. You know. The same."

"Haven't been there since you graduated college."

"Eight years ago."

"Has it already been that long?"

Tyler sipped his black coffee. He liked the bitterness. "Yep."

They continued to eat their meals, his father quickly devouring his platter. He reached up to signal for a refill. Pete returned with the pot. Tyler happily accepted being topped off. His eyes were still heavy with sleep from his unplanned early start to the day. His father pushed his empty plate in front of him and reclined into the booth. He watched Tyler carefully maneuver bites of his biscuits. He was so careful as not to miss a single drop, carefully packing the perfect bite into each forkful.

"So when's your flight back to New York? You said it's in a couple days."

"Yeah. About that. I don't know how to explain it. My place is still leased out for two months. And I kinda don't have a job at the moment. So I don't think I'm gonna make that return flight just yet." Tyler kept his eyes trained on his plate in front of him.

"That's a sound argument."

"I don't mean to put you in any sort of compromising

position. But could I please just stay with you for a bit? While I apply for some jobs."

"Absolutely," said his father. "But you gotta work on the farm while you do."

"That's fair. Thanks."

• • •

It was Tyler's second week at the house and he had picked up his father's habit of watching network sitcoms. Thursday nights meant a packed itinerary of *Mom*, *B Positive*, and *Young Sheldon*. Tyler never laughed, but it was something to look forward to. It was the only way he could mark the passing of time in those brutally dull days at the farm. His father was really loving that week's episode of *B Positive*. He laughed in a way Tyler had never known his father to laugh. He didn't even know his father could experience joy.

"You know, those laughs they play aren't even real, right," Tyler said as his father chuckled along. "It's a laugh track. Literally just an audio recording of people laughing that's layered on top of the scene. Nobody in that studio is laughing."

"Well, I'm laughing, ain't I?"

Fair point. Tyler turned back to the comedy of errors unraveling before him. The performances were actually not bad. Far less painful than sitcoms used to be. The late seasons of *Two and a Half Men* were particularly hard to stomach as his parents would watch in the living room as Tyler tried to drown out the noise in his bedroom.

"Did something happen with Leo?"

Tyler must've misheard. His father was probably referring to some character on the show.

"What was that?" asked Tyler. He wanted to clarify.

"Did something happen with Leo?" his father repeated. "Is that what all this is about?"

Tyler was breathless. He didn't know where to start. "Uh, you know Leo's name?"

"What kind of father doesn't know the name of the person his kid is living with?"

Tyler sat there. He had so much to say. He actually couldn't believe his father knew Leo's name. He couldn't believe his father had brought him up. He checked his father's face. There were no signs of malice, no signs of ill will. He looked at Tyler, waiting for a response. When a moment too long passed without speaking, his father jumped in.

"I'm sorry, I hope I didn't cross a line or anything—"

"No, no—you're fine! I was just collecting my... Leo was the catalyst for all of this. But it's not about him. Not really. I thought he was. I thought he was until recently. Leo left me. I worked too much. And I guess I drank—drink—too much. And it messed us up. We had a pretty incredible relationship, and I messed it up. I mean, he was there when Mom... And I never got past that. He was so good through so much, and I didn't repay him the favor. So after he left, I found this picture of me and Mom one summer in Michigan at the Traverse City Film Festival. It was that last summer before I left for college. And it was a picture of us at the premiere of *Eat Pray Love*. And we were so happy. We were hugging each other. And I think it was truly one of the best days of my life. And I wanted to feel that again. It was something so special—just between us. You can see how happy she was there! So I made a decision that day to re-create it. The movie, that is. I thought maybe if some woman out there could choose to uproot her entire life and career and go find her happiness and her purpose halfway across the world, then so could I. So I decided I would spend a month in Italy, then India, then Bali. But by the time I got to India, I ran out of money and had to hitchhike—or rather, *hike*—to the airport. Which leads me—"

"Here," his father said.

"Yes. Here. As if it were meant to be. Home. Maybe that's why they called me *Dorothy* on the playground."

His father laughed at his joke. He watched him process everything he had just told him. "Well," his father said evenly. "That's a lot."

"Yeah, I'll say."

"And you know what? I never even heard her talk about that movie..."

"Oh, that's because we didn't see it," said Tyler.

"Huh?"

"The movie. We didn't see it. Tickets sold out by the time we got up to the box office."

"But surely you rented it or something and watched it together later, right?"

"Nope."

His father burst out into an uncontrollable laughter. He covered his face, laughing into his palms as tears lined his face.

"You're telling me you did all the crap for a movie *you've never seen?!*"

"Well, I suppose it sounds a bit ridiculous when you put it like that."

"*Suppose?* Oh my goodness! That's so damn crazy!"

Tyler laughed a little bit at himself. "Yeah, I guess it is."

Tyler's chuckle grew to a full-blown laugh.

"Did you at least read the book?" his father managed to ask between bouts of laughter.

"Nope!" Tyler's laughter took over his body.

How good it was to laugh together, to break the tension that had existed between them for so long. And who wouldn't have laughed? The situation was entirely absurd. As their laughter died down, his father picked up the remote.

"Want to see if it's on Netflix?" he said.

"Ha! Sure," said Tyler.

His father found the movie and pressed play. He looked over at his father and half-smiled as they sat there watching *Eat Pray Love* for the first time.

•   •   •

Tyler sat in his room that night, the number already dialed into his phone. He didn't want to come off as crazy or needy. But he felt compelled to call. He paced back and forth, not sure whether to do it. At last, he clicked dial and listened as the phone rang. And rang. He hoped an answer wouldn't come. After the sixth ring, it went to voicemail. He waited for the beep, then spoke.

"Hey. I don't want to bother you. I just wanted to tell you something. I watched *Eat Pray Love* for the first time tonight. I know, hard to believe. Anyway. There's a scene where Julia Roberts goes into a meditation, hoping to heal from her heartbreak over James Franco, her ex-boyfriend. But instead, James doesn't show up. Her ex-husband, who she left, shows up: Billy Crudup. And to forgive herself for breaking her husband's heart, they dance to the song they were supposed to dance to at their wedding: *Harvest Moon*. Our song. You know, I'm always looking for a sign, so I took it as one. It really struck me, and it reminded me of all the hurt I caused. So, I wanted to apologize. I'm so sorry for not being the partner you deserved. You were so good to me, Leo. You really were. I hope you know how much I loved you. You deserve the best. Wherever you are, I hope you're doing great. I really do."

He hung up the phone and lay down.

• • •

He drove the tractor through the rows and rows of soybeans when his phone started buzzing. He had synced his phone to the tractor's Bluetooth system and had been blasting through Natalie Merchant's *Tigerlily*. The sound cut out just after the intro of *Carnival*, the beat replaced with the ringing of his phone.

"Hello!"

"Hey, Tyler," said his father. "Why don't you call it early today? I'm back here at the barn."

"Doesn't hurt my feelings!"

"Great."

Tyler hung up. He had no idea why his father was calling it quits early. It wasn't as if Tyler was doing an extraordinary job on the farm. In fact, the work he had done was fairly mediocre. He had driven the tractor painfully slowly through the fields, afraid of mucking up the growing crops. He guided the combine through the fields, back to the gravel road, then to the barn. He parked it outside, where his father stood next to his Ford F-150. He stepped out of the tractor and walked to his father.

"What's up?" asked Tyler.

"Let's hop in the truck. There's something you've gotta do."

"Alright. Are we going to a Garth Brooks concert or something?"

"Ha. You wish."

Tyler joined his father in the truck and buckled up. They pulled out and drove down the gravel road to the highway.

"So…" said Tyler, watching the highway pass by. "I've been thinking. On my trip, I made these friends. Who are from Paducah, of all places! And one woman in particular, she's single, and I don't know where you're at, but maybe you two could go meet up in Cape sometime for lunch if you'd like."

"Oh, cut that out," his father said. "I'm not ready for that stuff yet."

"Fine! Understandable. I was just thinking."

"And besides, what would a nice woman want with an old man like me?"

"She's truly one of the kindest people I've ever met," said Tyler.

"I'll consider it," his father said.

"Okay. That's all I ask."

They drove south through town. Tyler had no idea where they were headed. He looked at his old high school, just past the train tracks that divided the town. He saw the tennis court where he lost so many matches. His father cut across the Big Lots parking lot and made a left onto Main Street. As they drove, Tyler saw the cemetery growing closer. His father turned right onto the road that snaked through the cemetery. The pavement gave way to gravel as the car rolled to a stop.

"Oh, no. Please, no," Tyler begged. "I can't do this." His father placed his hand on his shoulder.

"It's time you do this."

Tyler exited the truck and stood for a moment. He looked at the green field littered with tombstones ahead of him. He wasn't sure where to go. He waited for his father to round the truck and lead the way. They walked quietly, respectfully out of the way of graves. After about fifty yards, his father came to a stop. He lowered his head. Tyler looked down and there it was amid the freshly grown grass: *Rebecca Morgan, Beloved Wife to Ed and Mother to Tyler.*

"I'll give you some privacy," his father said, walking back to the truck.

"Thank you."

Tyler stood there under that beautiful late July sun. The trees that bordered the cemetery were full of leaves that fluttered gently in the breeze. He looked down at the tombstone again. It pained him so to see her name there engraved in the marble: *Rebecca.* She had lived. Oh, she had lived. And she had been a good mother. She loved him more than he would ever know, he knew that. And she was down there.

"Hi, mom. I'm, I'm so sorry it's taken me so long to see you. Out here. I know you understand."

He paused to gather himself.

"Today has been two years since you died. Time sort of stopped for me that day. I think I was hoping that if I avoided—I don't know what I was thinking. I wasn't. Please don't be upset with me."

He stared at her tombstone, the words so succinct, so final. Etched into infinity. She was dead.

"I went on a trip. For you. Well, I thought it was supposed to be for me. But it was for you. And it was fun! Well, parts of it, at least. It did get challenging there at the end. I'd like to think you would've been proud of me. We were never super outdoorsy, me and you. But somehow, I got through it out there. I love you so much. I always will. All of these movies and books, they say that when you lose someone, you can feel that person with you. But I couldn't. Or, I didn't. So I kept thinking I needed to do more. Meet another person, and I'd feel you. Make another friend, and I'd see you. And I kept getting really close. And then my dreams. I couldn't escape it any longer. But it never happened—I never felt you. So I kept running. And now, I think it's because I haven't given myself the space and the time to feel you. I couldn't. It hurts too much. But I want you in my life. So I'm trying to be *still*—for once. I love you."

He wiped away his tears with his sleeve. He took a breath and looked to the sky. There wasn't a cloud to be found. The air was sweet with honeysuckle. He walked through the grass to where his father was. He took it in with deep breaths, feeling uplifted.

His father drove back to the farm. They didn't speak, yet it wasn't awkward. Looking around him, he felt that the town had a charm, a beauty he hadn't ever really noticed. It was almost quaint. *Almost.* He wondered why he had spent so much time hating it, denying it. He was tired of running from himself. He was exhausted. So much energy spent on blinding himself to the truth. He wanted no more of that.

Back at the barn with his father, Tyler unlocked the Camry. He wanted to go home and call Alexa. He knew he needed to apologize. He would make things right with her. And if he didn't, he would have at least tried. That was all he could do. The rest would be what was meant to be. And he was at peace with that.

"I love you, son."

Tyler stopped walking.

"What was that?" he asked.

His father held his gaze. He couldn't believe it. His chest swelled. "I love you, son!"

Tyler ran to his father. As he reached him, his father's arms extended open. He embraced him, wrapping his arms around his father's chest. Tyler let himself be hugged. He could feel how tightly his father held him. It was all he had ever wanted to hear.

"I love you, Dad!" he said. "I love you."

Tyler let himself cry there in his father's arms. His father tried his best to hold back his own tears but couldn't. It happened. The impossible had happened.

His father patted him on the back with one final squeeze before letting him go. They stood there with their arms at their hips, their faces wet with tears in the bright light of the day.

"I'm gonna go for a ride," said Tyler.

"That's just fine. I'll see you back at the house?"

"Yeah, I'll see you there."

He climbed into his mother's car and drove off. He wasn't sure where to go. There was nothing in town he was particularly interested in seeing, but that was okay. He would just drive. And he did. He drove all through town. He drove past the land where his grandparents had lived. Past the house where he had his first kiss. Past the salon where his mother took him as a child to get haircuts. And he smiled. He felt as if something had been lifted. Some heavy weight within him had seemingly vanished, taking with it so much.

He had no idea where he was going. He had no idea what he wanted to do. And yet, he felt at peace. He had a deep sense of knowing that he was exactly where he was supposed to be. It was an unfamiliar feeling. But it felt right. He trusted that he would find a job—that concern seemed so minuscule in the light of day. There would be heartbreaks. There would be love. There would be stress. There would be tears. There would be so much waiting for him. He stood on that precipice of potential.

More than anything, he wanted his mother there. And then he remembered: she was. He felt her. He saw her in the sun that shined. He recognized her in the smile of strangers. He heard her in the hum of life. She was around him then. She had always been with him. He just hadn't allowed himself to see that. The pain of her loss was unbearable. But the joy of her love was incomparable. It filled him and brought him to be. Janna was right: nothing is lost, only gained.

"I love you, Mom," he said as he drove.

He began to understand that his journey was his and his alone. It wasn't something to be copied or performed. It was as close to him as his breath, and even quieter. It was powerfully intimate—it held its power in that whisper. The whisper he heard months ago that had told him to get off the floor and *speak*. To *pray*. It was unlikely his journey would be committed to a book or adapted into a film. But not every journey was meant to be shared. This was his journey, his to learn from—alone—and no one could ever lead him from it.

He kept smiling. There was something so impossibly beautiful about the day. The road opened up before him. There was still so much to do. And God willing, so much time to experience it all. He had so much to be thankful for. He had been blessed beyond measure, and he had failed to recognize it for so long. He said a quiet prayer of gratitude as he drove. It was the first of its kind for Tyler. It felt good. He prayed for the past, and he prayed for the future. He prayed for those he knew, and he prayed for those he would eventually meet. He prayed for his mother. And he prayed for his father. *Amen*, he said to himself. *Amen.* He looked out at the sun setting just over the horizon. Tyler Morgan's life had just begun.

Acknowledgments

I have been blessed with the greatest parents a gal could ask for. Mom and Dad, I cannot thank you enough. You are unwavering towers of support, generosity, and love. Thank you, thank you, thank you. I love you both dearly, and I know that you love me *more than I can ever know*. You opened every door that I have walked through. I hope you can forgive the cursing and "adult content" in this book—it's for the sake of *art*! I would like to extend this thanks to the other members of my family: my brother Clinton D. and his wife Amy, my many cousins/family members, and to my grandmother "Bebe" Elizabeth Blaich. I love you all.

This book would not exist without the multitude of brilliant teachers and mentors who helped shape my voice and molded me into the writer I am today: Elissa Hogg, Janna Dooley, Gwendolyn Alker, Carol Sternhell, Kalle Westerling, Antonio Merenda, Jimmy Tripp, Jeanine Tesori, Jeff Talbott, Melissa Maxwell, the entire faculty of The Stella Adler Studio of Acting at NYU, Alithea Phillips, Alithea Phillips, and Alithea Phillips. Oh! And Alithea Phillips.

As any novice novelist is wont to do, I drew from my own experience within my own friendships when outlining and crafting this story. So, to my friends: THANK YOU! Austin McWilliams, my platonic other half and creative partner. Deirdre O'Toole, the brilliant woman who defines and redefines what a best friend is. Alexa Miller, Sophia Aronne, Grayce Toon, Max Weinstein, Ashley Eaker, Adam Lawrence, Joe Sullivan, Katie Gerber, Cinnamon Langley, Parker Smith, and Tyler Travers. And an extra special thanks to those of you who I forced to read earlier/terrible iterations of this novel and whose feedback was instrumental in getting this sucker published.

To Brandon Hoover, my hairstylist of eight years, and to Becca, my spray tanner of two years.

To RTH, thank you.

To John McMurtrie, my fabulous editor. You took a lump of clay and chiseled 'er down!

I would like to thank the women who lived their lives so fiercely and whose bodies of work continue to inspire me: Elizabeth Gilbert, Cheryl Strayed, Oprah Winfrey, Mary Tyler Moore, Bette Midler, Lucille Ball, Toni Morrison, Patti LuPone, Sandra Bernhard, and Phaedra Parks.

I played three albums *incessantly* when writing this novel: *Ray of Light* by Madonna, *Heard it in a Past Life* by Maggie Rogers, and *Eli and the Thirteenth Confession* by Laura Nyro. Thank you, divas.

I must thank my colleagues and work family at Atticus. I never dreamed I would find a job that energized me as much if not more than my creative work. Had this novel been published a year ago, I would have enough characters to list the entire team, but please know that I adore every single one of you and it is a privilege to work alongside you. Sam Byker, you are an endless fountain of knowledge, guidance, and friendship. I cannot thank you enough for taking a chance on me. Jackie Jakab, Jeni Popp, Ben Abrahams, Ben Gloger, Michael Behr (because you asked), Nin Nguyen, Connor Kreutz, Isabel Alison, and Maegan Seawright – thank you!

And finally, I would like to thank the two souls that make Los Angeles home: Romeo, who is all bark *and* all bite, and to Jacob Scott, a brilliant artist and the purest soul this side of creation. Despite having just written a book, my words are failing me as I'm faced with writing you a proper acknowledgment. So just know that I love you.

About the Author

DAVIS SUMMERS was born and raised in Poplar Bluff, Missouri. He obtained his BFA at New York University's Tisch School of the Arts. He resides in Los Angeles, CA.